444Rice Interrupted: A F

Copyright © 2026 by Tito Santos
(titosantos.mx@gmail.com)
All rights reserved.

All rights reserved. No part of this book may be reproduced, stored in a retrieval system, or transmitted in any form or by any means—electronic, mechanical, photocopying, recording, or otherwise—without the prior written permission of the publisher, except in the case of brief quotations embodied in critical reviews and certain other noncommercial uses permitted by copyright law.

This is a work of fiction. Names, characters, places, and incidents are either the product of the author's imagination or are used fictitiously. Any resemblance to actual persons, living or dead, events, or locales is entirely coincidental.

ISBN: 978-0-9983245-7-9 (paperback)

Holam Books and Media

First Edition

Rice Interrupted: A Farmer's Fate

Tito Santos

Rice Interrupted: A Farmer's Fate

Table of Contents

Foreword

Dedication

Part One: The Leaving

Chapter 1: The Leaving

Chapter 2: The Hundred-Thousand-Peso Man

Chapter 3: The Translator's Smile

Chapter 4: The Golden Jail

Chapter 5: The Parable of the Two Assistants

Part Two: The Falling

Chapter 6: The Umbrella Girl and the Golf Game

Chapter 7: The Proposal and the Mother's Teeth

Chapter 8: The Vanishing and the Twin

Chapter 9: The Nostalgia Trap

Part Three: The Unraveling

Chapter 10: The Society of Women

Chapter 11: A Taste of Paradise

Chapter 12: The Wake

Afterword

Appendix

347

Character Study: The Names We Carry
Haiku

The Disease We Pass Down: A Meditation on Violence and the Golden Rule

Acknowledgment: Margie's Legacy

About the Author

Dedication

For Bella, Derek, and Niko—
you are the friendship I was walking toward before I
knew I needed friends.

For my beloved cousin Kellia—
blood of my blood, heart of my heart,
the one who remembers with me.

And for my friends across the diaspora—
scattered like seeds from the same tree,
growing in strange soil,
still reaching toward the same sun.

This story is a warning, a memory, a prayer.
It is for you.
It is because of you.
It is, in the end, all I have to give.

May we find homes that do not become graves.

May we find loves that do not become traps.

May we find peace, and know it when we see it.

Foreword

This is a work of fiction. The characters, their names, their stories, their deaths—all of it is imagined, invented, made from the cloth of possibility rather than the thread of fact.

And yet.

The man in these pages is not entirely a stranger to me. I have known him in the shadows of other men's stories, in the quiet confessions of friends and strangers, in the news reports that flicker across screens and then vanish into the endless stream of forgetting. He is the Black American who goes looking for freedom and finds something else. He is the dreamer who builds a kingdom on someone else's land. He is the lover who discovers that love, in some hands, is just another weapon.

I moved to the Philippines in the late 2000s, fleeing the same America that Norman Wright flees in these pages. I knew the traffic stops, the overqualified verdicts, the slow suffocation of being Black in a country that was built on my ancestors' bones and has never stopped reminding me of it. I knew the hope that blooms when you step off a plane and discover that your money, suddenly, is enough. That you, suddenly, are enough.

I knew the rice fields too. The farmer who took me in, who spoke no English but spoke welcome in a language older than words. His daughter, who translated the world for me and, in doing so, gave me the greatest gift one human can give another: the truth of being seen.

The rest of this story—the women, the twins, the scams, the mansions, the poison—that part is invented. But the shape of it, the architecture of trust and betrayal, the slow realization that the people smiling at you might be counting your money in their heads—that shape is real. I have seen it. I have heard it from others who lived it. I have sat in bars and on beaches and in cheap restaurants and listened to men tell their versions of this story, their voices caught somewhere between laughter and tears.

This book is for them. For the ones who survived and the ones who didn't. For the ones who came looking for paradise and found something that looked like it, felt like it, tasted like it—until it didn't.

And it is for Norman. Poor, hopeful, doomed Norman. He wanted what we all want. To be loved. To belong. To matter. He found it, for a while, or thought he did. And in the end, that was enough to kill him.

The mystery you are about to read is not just about who killed Norman Wright. It is about why he was killable in the first place. About the loneliness that makes us vulnerable. About the hope that makes us blind. About the history we carry in our bones, a low-grade fever that never quite breaks.

The answers, such as they are, lie ahead.

Read on. But remember: the most beautiful places can be graves. And the people who love you may be the ones digging it.

— The Author

Chapter 1: The Leaving

The apartment was a coffin with a window unit.

Norman Wright sat on the edge of his bed, the springs groaning under a weight that wasn't just his own. Outside, the Chicago evening was doing its summer thing—thick, loud, the smell of grilled meat and exhaust fumes wrestling in the air. He could hear the distant yelp of a police siren, a sound so common it had become a kind of silence. He didn't move. He just listened to the hum of the refrigerator, a sound like a trapped insect, and watched the dust motes dance in the slants of dying sun.

Fifty-eight years. It felt like a sentence you served for a crime you couldn't remember committing.

The job interview that afternoon had been a masterclass in humiliation. A young white man with a firm handshake and eyes that never quite landed on Norman's face had scanned his resume like it was written in a foreign language. "Overqualified," he'd said, for the fourth time this year. It was the polite word. The word they used when they saw a Black man with a lifetime of experience and decided he was too much, too heavy, too something for their bright, open-plan office. Norman had smiled, nodded, and felt the familiar weight settle deeper into his bones, a sediment of 347 years.

He thought of his father, a steelworker who came home with burns on his arms and a quiet dignity in his eyes. A man who voted every election like it was a sacred duty, who taught Norman to keep his hands on the steering wheel at all times, to never make sudden movements. "They ain't looking for a reason, son," he'd say, his voice a low rumble. "They're looking for an excuse." His father had died of a heart attack at sixty-two, worn down by work and the slow poison of a thousand small deferrals.

The memory brought him to his feet. He walked to the window and looked down at the street. A squad car was parked at the corner, two officers inside, their faces glowing blue from a dashboard screen. Just waiting. Just watching. He remembered the last time they'd watched him. A traffic stop six months ago. A taillight was out. He'd done everything right—hands on the wheel, engine off, movements slow. The officer, a kid with a crew cut and a hand on his holster, had still screamed at him to get out of the car, had still thrown him against the hot hood and patted him down like he was disarming a bomb. For a taillight.
They'd let him go with a warning. No apology. Just the metallic taste of fear in his mouth and the echo of his father's voice in his head.

He turned from the window. The apartment was small, but it contained the sum total of his American life. A few books by Baldwin and Ellison. A faded photograph of his mother. A stack of rejection letters and final notices. It was the architecture of a trap, a cage built not of bars but of ceilings. Invisible ceilings on promotions. Invisible ceilings on loans. Invisible ceilings on his very breath, a ceiling that could come crashing down at any moment, for any reason, or for no reason at all. The news was full of it. Men who looked like him, breathed like him, were being killed for selling loose cigarettes, for reaching for their licenses, for simply existing while Black. And the men who killed them walked. They walked with paychecks and pensions, their faces placid on the evening news.

The ticket to Manila was on the dresser. A one-way ticket. He'd bought it three weeks ago, in a fit of desperate hope, and had looked at it every day since, a talisman against the despair. The Philippines. He'd read about it online. A place where the exchange rate made you rich. A place where the color of his skin might not be the first and last thing people saw. A place where a Black man could just be a man.

He picked up the ticket. The paper was smooth, flimsy. It felt like a promise.

He thought of his ancestors, brought here in chains, forced to build a nation that would never truly see them. He thought of his grandparents, who fled the Jim Crow South (where Blacks could not use the same toilet as white people) for the promised land of the North, only to find a new kind of crow, just as mean, just as hungry. He thought of his own life, a testament to survival, but not to living. He was a leaf on a river of blood, carried along by a current he couldn't see and couldn't fight.

The siren outside grew louder, then faded into the night.

Norman put the ticket in his pocket. He didn't pack a suitcase. He just took a small bag, his wallet, his passport. He left the apartment key on the kitchen counter. He didn't lock the door on his way out. What was there left to steal?

The taxi ride to O'Hare was a blur of lights and expressways. He watched the city recede in the rearview mirror, a jagged skyline against the bruised purple sky. He felt a strange, hollow lightness, as if he'd left his organs back in that apartment. He was a husk, a man-shaped thing, moving towards an unknown shore.

At the check-in counter, the agent, a young woman with a kind smile, took his passport. She flipped through it, stamped a page, and handed it back.

"Enjoy your stay in the Philippines, Mr. Wright," she said.

Stay. The word was a small, sad joke. He wasn't going for a stay. He was going for a life.

He walked through the security checkpoint, past the tired families and the busy businessmen, and onto the jet bridge. The plane's engine hummed, a deep, mechanical heartbeat. He found his seat by the window and buckled himself in. As the plane taxied down the runway, he pressed his forehead against the cool glass and looked out at the city he was leaving behind. The lights of Chicago sparkled in the darkness, beautiful and indifferent. A necklace of diamonds on the throat of a ghost.

Then the plane lifted off, and the city fell away. The lights blurred, shrank, and were swallowed by the clouds.

He was leaving. He was escaping. He was, for the first time in his life, choosing the unknown over the known.

But as the plane climbed higher, a thought settled into him, not heavy like the old sediment, but persistent, like a low-grade fever you learn to live with. It was a question without an answer, a splinter in the mind. He closed his eyes and let the hum of the engines carry him east, into the dark, towards the rising sun.

End-of-Chapter Question: Can a man ever truly escape the history that shaped him, or does he carry it in his bones like a low-grade fever?

Chapter 2: The Hundred-Thousand-Peso Man

The plane descended through a wall of white clouds and then, suddenly, there it was: Manila. It spread out below him like a wound that had healed wrong—brown, dense, pulsing. Norman pressed his forehead to the cold plastic of the window and watched the city rise up to meet him. Thousands of corrugated tin roofs, a maze of narrow streets, the lazy curl of smoke from a hundred unseen fires. The plane bumped and shuddered and then they were on the ground, the engines reversing with a great mechanical roar that sounded, to Norman, like the exhalation of a giant.

The air hit him first. It was not air as he knew it. It was a wet, warm blanket, thick with the smell of diesel, frying bananas, and something sweet and floral he couldn't name. It wrapped around him, pressed against his skin, seeped into his lungs. He walked through the jet bridge, his small bag slung over his shoulder, and followed the crowd into the terminal.

The noise was a physical force. A thousand conversations in a language he didn't understand, the clatter of luggage carts, the tinny pop music leaking from overhead speakers, the insistent calls of taxi drivers herding passengers like sheep. He felt untethered, a cork bobbing on a choppy sea. Then he saw the currency exchange counter.

He waited in line, watching the people around him. Families reunited with tearful embraces. Young white men with backpacks and sunburns. Filipinos in crisp business attire, moving with purpose. When it was his turn, he pushed his meager savings across the counter—dollars he had hoarded for years, the grave dirt of his American life.

The woman behind the counter counted it with efficient fingers, then pushed a thick stack of Philippine pesos back at him. He stared at the pile of bills. It was more cash than he had held in his entire life. Thousand-peso notes, five-hundred-peso notes, a rainbow of color and possibility. He was, in the space of a single transaction, a multimillionaire.

The word felt ridiculous in his head. Multimillionaire. He, Norman Wright, son of a steelworker, grandson of a sharecropper, a man who had spent his life being told he was too much and not enough, was now a rich man. By doing nothing. By simply crossing a border. The absurdity of it made him want to laugh, but the laugh got caught in his throat. It was too big, too strange, too laced with a bitter irony he couldn't yet name.

His contact, a friend of a friend named Boyet, was waiting for him outside the arrivals hall, holding a sign that said "NORMAN WELCOME." Boyet was a small man with a huge smile and eyes that crinkled when he talked. He pumped Norman's hand like he was drawing water from a well.

"Sir Norman! Welcome, welcome, welcome to the Philippines!" Boyet's English was rapid and musical. "You are here! Finally! How was the flight? Long, yes? Very long. Come, come, the car is this way. We have a long drive. You will see the real Philippines."

The vehicle was a tricycle, a motorcycle attached to a handmade cab amidst jeepney transports, a decorated vehicle that looked like it had been assembled from the remains of a World War II army jeep and a carnival float. Norman climbed into the front seat, his knees nearly touching his chin, and they lurched into the legendary Manila traffic. Boyet talked the entire time, pointing out landmarks Norman couldn't see through the haze and the chaos. He talked about his family, about the rice farms in the north, about the beauty of the provincial life.

Norman stopped listening. He was watching out the open side of the vehicle, watching the city stream by. He saw children begging at stopped cars, their faces smudged with dirt, their hands outstretched. He saw women in neat uniforms stepping out of gleaming office towers. He saw a man sleeping on a cardboard mat on a traffic island, undisturbed by the river of metal flowing around him. He saw shanties built so close to the highway he could have reached out and touched their tin walls, and behind them, the glass-and-steel condominiums of the wealthy, rising like monuments to a different world.

The poverty was not abstract. It was not a statistic in a report. It was right there, in the brown eyes of a child pressing his face to the window, in the tired slump of a woman selling cigarettes by the roadside. It was raw and real and it made Norman's new wealth feel strange, almost shameful. He was a millionaire in a country where a million pesos could buy a house but a few coins could buy a child's meal.

They left the city as the sun began to set, crawling through the sprawl until the buildings thinned and the green began to assert itself. The air changed, losing some of its diesel bite and gaining the sweet smell of vegetation. Boyet fell into a comfortable silence, humming along to a song on the radio.

Hours later, under a canopy of stars so thick and bright they looked like spilled salt, they turned onto a dirt road. The tricycle bumped and swayed through the darkness, past sleeping houses and barking dogs. Finally, they stopped.

"We are here, Sir Norman," Boyet said. "My family's home."

Norman climbed out, his legs stiff, his body humming with exhaustion. The night air was cool and clean. He could hear the chirping of insects, a sound like a million tiny violins. And then, as his eyes adjusted, he saw it.

The rice field.

It stretched out before him, a vast, dark expanse under the moonlight. But it was not dark, not really. The rising moon painted the tops of the rice stalks with silver, turning the field into a shimmering sea of liquid light. The water between the paddies reflected the stars, so that it seemed he was standing at the edge of two skies—one above, one below. A soft breeze moved through the stalks, a whispering sound, like the breath of the earth itself.

He had never seen anything so beautiful. He had never seen anything so peaceful. He had never seen anything so utterly foreign to the world he had left behind.

A figure emerged from a small nipa hut, a man with a weathered face and a slow, deliberate walk. He said nothing, just looked at Norman with calm, appraising eyes. Then he nodded, once, and gestured towards the hut.

This was the farmer. This was the man whose family would take him in. This was the beginning.

Norman stood there for a long moment, caught between the weight of his American past and the shimmering promise of this Philippine night. He was a rich man in a poor man's world. He was a stranger in a place that felt, for the first time in his life, like a possibility. He looked up at the impossible stars and felt the low-grade fever of his history thrum quietly in his blood.

But for now, it was quiet. For now, it was just him and the field and the silent farmer, waiting.

End-of-Chapter Question: When you become rich simply by crossing a border, is the wealth real, or is it just a trick of the light, a mirage that can vanish just as fast?

Chapter 3: The Translator's Smile

Morning came not with an alarm but with light. It poured through the gaps in the bamboo walls of the nipa hut, golden and insistent, painting stripes across the dirt floor. Norman lay on a thin mattress, his body sore from the tricycle ride, his mind still tangled in the strange threads of half-remembered dreams. He could hear movement outside, the cluck of chickens, the low murmur of voices.

He sat up and looked around the small room. It was spare, simple. A few clothes hung on nails. A crucifix above the door. A photograph of a wedding, yellowed with age, pinned to the wall. This was not a hotel. This was a home. He was a guest in the truest sense, a stranger trusted by people who had nothing.

He pulled on his shirt and stepped outside.

The scene before him was a painting he wished he had the skill to capture. The rice field stretched to the hills in the distance, a thousand shades of green under the morning sun. The farmer, whose name he still did not know, was already in the field, standing knee-deep in the muddy water, his back curved like a question mark as he tended to the young plants. He moved slowly, methodically, with the patience of a man who understood that the earth could not be hurried.

Near the hut, a woman was feeding chickens, scattering grain from a worn basket. She glanced at Norman, smiled quickly, and looked away. A young girl, maybe ten years old, was pumping water from a hand pump into a plastic bucket, her thin arms working with a practiced rhythm.

And then he saw her.

She was walking up the path from the field, a book tucked under her arm. She wore a simple dress, faded but clean, and her feet were bare, dusty from the path. Her hair was pulled back, revealing a high forehead and intelligent eyes that found him immediately, assessed him, and then softened into a smile.

"You must be Norman," she said. Her English was clear, precise, accented but perfect. "I'm Maria. My father said you arrived last night. I hope you slept well."

Her father. The farmer. Of course.

"I slept better than I have in years," Norman said, and was surprised to find it was true. "Thank you for letting me stay."

Maria laughed, a sound like small bells. "It is our pleasure. We do not have many visitors, especially not from America. My father is shy. He does not speak English. But he is happy you are here. He told me to tell you that his home is your home."

She gestured for him to follow and led him to a small table set under a mango tree. A woman, presumably her mother, brought out plates of rice, fried fish, and sliced mangoes. Maria sat with him, translating the silent offerings of her family into a running commentary.

"My mother wants to know if the food is okay. She is worried it is too simple for an American."
"Tell her it's perfect. Better than any restaurant I've ever eaten in."

Maria translated, and the mother's face bloomed with a shy, proud smile.

That first day was a revelation. Maria became his guide, his teacher, his window into a world he could not have imagined. She walked him through the rice field, explaining the cycle of planting and harvest, the delicate balance of water and sun. She showed him the carabao, the great water buffalo that lounged in a muddy pond like a living monument to patience. She told him the names of plants and birds, the superstitions of her grandmother, the stories carved into the landscape by generations of her family.

"You have education," Norman said, noticing again the book she carried. It was a textbook, dog-eared and well-read. "You're studying."

"I am studying business at the university in the city," she said, a flicker of something—pride? longing?—crossing her face. "I go when I can. When there is money for the bus. When my family does not need me here."

"That must be hard."

She looked out at the field, at her father's distant figure. "It is harder to stay," she said quietly. "My mother and father, they are good people. They work so hard. But this life…" She gestured at the field, the hut, the whole of the provincial world. "It is beautiful, yes. But it is a trap. There is no money. There is no future. The young people, they all go to the city. Or they go abroad, to work as maids, as sailors, as anything. They send money home. That is how families survive."

Norman listened. He heard the echo of his own people in her words, the same story told in a different key. The land as love, the land as cage. The young fleeing, the old remaining, the money from faraway places keeping the whole fragile thing from collapsing.

Over the following days, a rhythm established itself. Norman helped where he could, though his city hands were useless in the field. He fetched water, swept the yard, played with the younger children. He sat with the farmer in the evenings, saying nothing, sharing the comfortable silence of men who had learned that words were not always necessary. And he talked with Maria. They talked for hours. About America, about the Philippines, about race and history and the strange, cruel ways the world sorted its people. He told her about Chicago, about his father, about the traffic stop and the job interviews and the slow, suffocating weight of being Black in America. She listened with an intensity that made him feel seen, truly seen, for the first time in years.

"It is the same here," she said one evening, as the sun bled orange and red into the rice field. "Not the same, but the same shape. The poor are poor because their parents were poor. The powerful stay powerful because they own the laws. We have our own history of slavery, our own masters. The names are different, but the feeling…" She touched her chest. "It is the same here."

He looked at her, this young woman with the bare feet and the textbook and the eyes that had seen too much for her years. He felt a warmth that was more than friendship, a pull towards her intelligence, her spirit, her quiet strength. He began to imagine something. A partnership. A romance. A future where he wasn't alone.

One evening, under the mango tree, he tried to tell her. He spoke carefully, awkwardly, about how much her friendship meant to him, how he felt a connection he hadn't felt in a long time. He talked about the possibility of something more.

She listened. Her face was kind, patient. And when he was done, she reached out and touched his hand, gently, briefly.

"Norman," she said softly. "You are a good man. A kind man. And I am honored to be your friend. But I am not for you. Not in that way."

He felt the sting, but it was a clean sting, a wound without poison.

"I have dreams," she continued. "I want to go to the city. I want to finish my education. I want to build a life that will lift my family out of this poverty. A man, a husband, a family of my own… that will come later. But first, I must become myself. Do you understand?"

He did understand. How could he not? He had spent his whole life fighting to become himself, and America had spent his whole life telling him he wasn't allowed.

"I'm sorry," he said. "I didn't mean to—"

"No," she said, cutting him off. "Do not be sorry. You honored me with your honesty. And you gave me a gift." She smiled, that bell-like sound. "You treated me like an equal. Like a person. Not many men do that here. Not even the young ones."

They sat in silence as the stars emerged, one by one, over the rice field. The warmth between them had changed, shifted into something else, something perhaps deeper than romance could ever be. It was friendship. True friendship, unburdened by wanting.

Later that night, as he lay on his mattress listening to the insect chorus, Norman thought about what she had said. She was seeking freedom, just as he had been. Her cage was poverty and provincial expectation. His cage had been the color of his skin and the weight of history. They were two birds, perched on different branches, singing different songs, but both longing for the same sky.

He fell asleep with the image of her smile in his mind, and for the first time since arriving, the low-grade fever of his history seemed to ease, just a little.

End-of-Chapter Question: Is the purest connection with another person the one you don't try to possess, and is that why it hurts the most to let it go?

Chapter 4: The Golden Jail

The immigration officer at the Cebu City office had the tired eyes of a man who spent his days saying no to people. He studied Norman's passport, flipped through the pages, looked at the visa extension form, and then looked at Norman with an expression that was not quite suspicion but not quite welcome either.

"Six months," the officer said. "Then you report again. Every two months. You understand the requirements?"

Norman understood. He was a guest in this country, a temporary resident, a man whose presence was tolerated but not guaranteed. The stamp in his passport was a reminder: you do not belong here. Not really. Not yet.

He walked out of the immigration office and into the furnace of a Cebu City afternoon. The sun was a white-hot coin in a pale sky, and the air was thick with the smell of exhaust and frying food and the sweet, cloying scent of overripe mangoes. A pack of tricycle drivers descended on him immediately, their vehicles—motorcycles with attached sidecars, brightly painted and decorated with religious icons and stickers of movie stars—jostling for position.

"Sir! Sir! Where you go?"
"Best price, sir! I take you!"
"Air-conditioned! Very cold!"

Norman picked one, a young guy with a gap-toothed smile and a rosary hanging from his rearview mirror, and gave him the address of the condo he had rented online. The tricycle lurched into traffic, weaving between cars and buses and other tricycles with a daring that made Norman's heart stutter. The driver, whose name was Junjun, talked constantly, pointing out landmarks Norman couldn't track, complaining about the traffic, asking Norman where he was from, if he was married, if he liked Filipino food.

It was chaos. It was beautiful. It was nothing like the provincial quiet he had left behind.

The condo building rose from the chaos like a glass monument to another world. A uniformed guard opened the door for him. The lobby was cool and marble and utterly silent. Norman rode the elevator to the twentieth floor, walked down a carpeted hallway, and unlocked the door to his new home.

The apartment was small but perfect. Polished concrete floors. Floor-to-ceiling windows overlooking the city and the sea beyond. A kitchen with appliances he didn't know how to use. A bed the size of his entire Chicago apartment. He walked to the window and pressed his palm against the glass. Below him, the city seethed and sweltered. Above him, the air conditioning hummed, a cool, mechanical breath.

He was living better than any white man who had ever denied him a job. Better than the cop who had thrown him against the hood of his own car. Better than the HR manager with the overqualified verdict. The thought should have been satisfying. It should have been a victory, a vindication, a middle finger raised to the entire architecture of American racism.

But standing there, looking down at the tiny tricycles and the tiny people and the tiny lives unfolding in the heat, Norman felt something else entirely. He felt alone.

The first week was a blur of acquisition. He bought furniture. He bought clothes. He bought a television so large it made his Chicago apartment look like a dollhouse. He hired a cleaner, a shy woman named Nita who came twice a week and refused to call him anything but "Sir." He opened a bank account, and the manager treated him like royalty, offering him coffee and a comfortable chair and a special account for people with "substantial deposits."

Money in this city was a key that opened every door. Restaurant tables appeared when he walked in. Taxis stopped when he raised his hand. Women smiled at him on the street, in the malls, in the coffee shops where he sat and watched the world go by. He was not blind. He knew what those smiles meant, or could mean. He was a foreigner, a rich man, a prize to be won.

But the loneliness persisted. It was there in the morning when he woke up in his huge bed and reached for a warmth that wasn't there. It was there in the evening when he watched the sunset from his window, the sky turning the same colors as over the rice field, but somehow less beautiful, less real. It was there in the quiet moments between acquisitions, between transactions, between the small, meaningless victories of his new life.

He thought about Maria. He wondered if she had made it to the city yet, if she was sitting in a classroom somewhere, chasing her dreams with that quiet, fierce determination. He thought about her smile, her laughter, the way she had touched his hand and let him down gently. She had given him the gift of friendship, and he had left it behind in a rice field. He could call her. He could visit. But something held him back. Some fear that the connection had been tied to that place, to those evenings under the mango tree, and that bringing it here, to this glass-and-steel world, would somehow diminish it.

One evening, sitting in a rooftop bar surrounded by expats and business travelers and young Filipino women in expensive dresses, Norman made a decision. He pulled out his phone and downloaded a dating app. The icon appeared on his screen, a little flame, a promise of connection.

A friend from the condo, a retired Australian named Dave, had given him advice over too many San Miguel beers. "You'll date a dozen, maybe fifteen, before you find the right one, mate. That's just how it works here. The women, they're beautiful, they're lovely, but you gotta find the one who loves you for you, not for your passport or your pension. It's a minefield. But it's a fun minefield, if you know what I mean."

Norman didn't know what he meant, not really. But he was lonely. And the app was there. And the women were there, a gallery of smiling faces, each one a possibility, each one a potential cure for the emptiness that had taken up residence in his twentieth-floor apartment.

He swiped right on the first one. Then the second. Then the third.

The golden jail was comfortable. It was beautiful. It had a view of the sea. But it was still a jail, and Norman was still a prisoner, locked in with nothing but his money and his memories and the low-grade fever that never quite went away.

End-of-Chapter Question: When you finally get everything you ever wanted, why does it feel so much like a beautifully decorated cage?

Chapter 5: The Parable of the Two Assistants

The idea came to him in the shallow hours of the night, when sleep wouldn't come and the city lights below his window painted the ceiling in shifting colors. He was tired of being just a man with money. He was tired of the emptiness that acquisitions couldn't fill. He needed to build something. He needed to work.

Digital consulting. It was vague enough to mean anything and specific enough to sound impressive. He had spent thirty years in the margins of American business—middle management, project coordination, the kind of jobs that kept you alive but never let you thrive. He knew how companies worked, how systems functioned, how to solve problems that other people couldn't see. Surely that was worth something here.

He ran the idea past Dave, the Australian, over beers at the rooftop bar. Dave nodded enthusiastically, his sunburned face gleaming under the string lights.

"Brilliant, mate. Absolutely brilliant. There's tons of small businesses here, family shops, export companies, they're all desperate to get online, to modernize, but they don't know how. And the locals, they're smart, don't get me wrong, but they don't have the big-picture thinking. You could clean up."

Norman didn't want to clean up. He just wanted to matter.

He found office space in a commercial building not far from his condo—a small room with air conditioning and windows that looked out on a wall, but it was enough. He registered the business, a surprisingly simple process when you had money and a friendly fixer to handle the paperwork. And then he needed staff.

The job posting attracted dozens of applicants. Young Filipinos, mostly women, with college degrees and hopeful eyes and resumes that listed English proficiency and computer skills and a desperate willingness to learn. Norman interviewed them all, sitting behind a borrowed desk, feeling like a fraud and a king in equal measure.

Two stood out.

The first was Rosalie. She was quiet, almost shy, with wire-rimmed glasses and a nervous habit of tucking her hair behind her ear. Her resume was solid, her English was excellent, and she looked at Norman with an earnestness that bordered on reverence. She came from a province in the south, she explained, the eldest of six children, the first in her family to graduate college. She needed this job. Her family needed her to need this job.

The second was Charmaine. She was everything Rosalie was not—loud, confident, dressed in clothes that seemed slightly too expensive for someone applying for an entry-level position. She laughed easily, talked rapidly, and had a way of looking at Norman that suggested she already knew everything about him and found it amusing. Her resume was fine, nothing special, but her personality filled the room like smoke.

Norman hired them both. Rosalie for her competence, her quiet reliability, the feeling that she would never cause him trouble. Charmaine because she made him laugh, and laughter was in short supply in his golden jail.

The first month was good. The business grew slowly, steadily. Norman landed a few small contracts—a travel agency that needed a better website, a furniture exporter who wanted to reach American buyers, a local restaurant chain that needed help with their online ordering system. Rosalie handled the details, the spreadsheets, the follow-up emails, with a quiet efficiency that Norman came to rely on. Charmaine handled the clients, charming them with her laugh and her confidence, making them feel like they were getting more than they paid for.

They worked well together, the quiet one and the loud one. Norman allowed himself to feel proud. He was building something. He was creating jobs, contributing to the economy, proving that he was more than just a rich foreigner with a nice condo.

The first hint of trouble came two months in. Norman noticed a discrepancy in the petty cash. A small amount, barely worth noting, but it bothered him. He checked the records, found nothing conclusive, and let it go. Then it happened again. A little more this time. He mentioned it to both women, casually, without accusation. Rosalie's face went pale, and she assured him she would be more careful with the records. Charmaine laughed it off, said it was probably just a mistake, these things happen.

Norman wanted to believe them. He needed to believe them.

He started watching more carefully. Not openly—he didn't want to seem like a suspicious boss, an ugly American assuming the worst of the people who worked for him. But he paid attention. He noticed that Charmaine had started arriving late, her usual brightness dimmed, her eyes sometimes unfocused. He noticed that Rosalie had become even quieter, even more diligent, as if she was trying to compensate for something.

Then the real money disappeared.

A client had paid a substantial deposit, cash, for a big project. Norman had left it in his office safe, planning to deposit it the next day. When he opened the safe, the money was gone. Not all of it—whoever had taken it had left enough to make the theft less obvious, a careful, calculated amount.

He sat at his desk, staring at the remaining bills, and felt the familiar weight settle into his bones. The weight of betrayal. The weight of being fooled. The weight of his own stupidity.

He called them both into his office. He didn't accuse. He just stated the facts. The money was missing. The safe had been locked. Only three people knew the combination.

Charmaine's reaction was immediate and dramatic. Tears, denials, accusations that it must have been Rosalie, that quiet ones were always the sneaky ones, that she couldn't believe Norman would suspect her, her, who had worked so hard, who had brought in so many clients.
Rosalie said nothing. She sat perfectly still, her hands folded in her lap, her face a mask of calm that Norman later realized was the calm of someone who had already been convicted and was simply waiting for the sentence.

He investigated. It didn't take long. A neighbor near Rosalie's boarding house, paid a small amount for information, told him about the visitors, the late-night parties, the strange men who came and went at all hours. A landlord who had evicted a previous tenant for the same thing identified the signs. Shabu. The local meth. Cheap, destructive, everywhere.

The quiet one. The trustworthy one. The one he had trusted completely. She had been hooked for months, maybe since before he hired her. The small discrepancies, the gradual decline, the desperate need for money—it all made sense now. Charmaine, for all her flaws, was clean. Rosalie, the one he had believed in, was the thief.

He fired her. She didn't fight it. She didn't cry. She just nodded, gathered her things, and walked out of his office without a word. Charmaine watched her go, and for a moment, her usual bravado slipped, and Norman saw something else underneath. Fear, maybe. Or relief that it hadn't been her.

Later that week, Norman sat alone in his office, the city humming outside his window, and thought about what had happened. He had been so sure. He had looked at Rosalie's quiet dignity, her hard work, her desperate need, and he had seen a reflection of himself. Someone who deserved a chance. Someone who would never betray a kindness.

He had been wrong. The quiet ones could be hiding anything. The desperate ones would do desperate things. And the person who needed you most might also be the person who would destroy you without a second thought.

He thought about Maria, the translator, the only person in this country who had shown him kindness with no string attached. He thought about how easily he had left her behind, how quickly he had replaced the peace of the rice field with the glitter of the city. He thought about the women on the dating app, the parade of smiling faces, each one a potential Rosalie or Charmaine, each one a mystery he couldn't solve.
The money was gone. It didn't matter—he had plenty more. But the trust was gone too, and that was harder to replace. The low-grade fever of his history had found new fuel, new proof that the world was what he had always suspected it was. A place where the biggest dangers wore the most innocent faces.

End-of-Chapter Question: When someone shows you who they are, do you have the courage to believe them, or does your own hope make you an easy mark?

Chapter 6: The Umbrella Girl and the Golf Game

The parade continued.

After Rosalie, after the betrayal, after the quiet office became a place of ghosts and memories, Norman threw himself into the distraction of companionship with a kind of desperate determination. The app became his companion, his confessor, his carnival barker. He swiped and matched and messaged and met, a revolving door of women who arrived with smiles and left with polite excuses or, occasionally, with hope that flickered and died.

There was Elena, the nurse, who talked about her ex-husband for three hours and cried into her pasta. There was Jasmine, the call center agent, who asked about his finances on the first date and his intentions on the second. There was Maricel, the teacher, who was kind and gentle and so profoundly boring that Norman found himself praying for the check to arrive. There was Girlie, the entrepreneur, who tried to sell him a timeshare. There was Lorna, the widow, who looked at him with hungry eyes and made him feel like a meal.

Twelve. Thirteen. Fourteen. Dave's prediction was proving accurate, if not optimistic. Norman dated them all, learned their stories, bought them dinners, listened to their dreams. Some he saw twice. Most he saw once. None of them touched the loneliness. None of them made the fever ease.

Number eighteen was Lilette.

Her profile photo showed a young woman in an umbrella girl uniform—the bright polo shirt, the visor, the smile that was part of a job requirement and part of something else. She worked at the golf course, the fancy one up in the hills where the expats played and the wealthy Filipinos closed business deals over eighteen holes. Her bio was simple: "I like nature and smiling. Looking for serious relationship."

Norman swiped right without much thought. Another face. Another possibility. Another chance to be disappointed.

They met for dinner at a restaurant near her home, a place that served decent Filipino food and cold beer. She arrived on time, which was rare, and she was prettier than her photos, which was rarer still. Small, fine-boned, with short hair cut boyishly close to her head and a smile that seemed to start in her eyes. She wore jeans and a simple blouse, no makeup that Norman could see, and she ordered without hesitation, which he appreciated.

The conversation was pleasant. She talked about her work at the golf course, the rich foreigners she caddied for, the tips that made the job worthwhile. She talked about her family, her mother, her siblings, but skipped over details with a practiced vagueness that Norman recognized from his own conversations about America. Some things you don't share with strangers. Some things you keep close.

She asked about him. He gave the edited version—Chicago, the move, the business, the condo. He didn't mention the loneliness. He didn't mention the fever. He didn't mention Rosalie or the betrayal or the quiet desperation that had brought him to this restaurant, to this table, to this woman with the short hair and the careful smile.

When the meal ended, he paid the bill and walked her to a tricycle. She thanked him politely, said she had a nice time, and disappeared into the neon chaos of the city night. Norman stood on the sidewalk for a long moment, watching the tricycle's taillights fade, and felt nothing. She was nice. She was pretty. But something was off. A distance behind her eyes. A wall he couldn't see but could feel.

He decided not to contact her again.

A week passed. Two weeks. The parade continued. Number nineteen was a marketing manager who talked endlessly about her dogs. Number twenty was a dentist who kept examining his teeth during dinner. Norman was starting to think Dave's numbers were optimistic, that

maybe the right one didn't exist, that maybe he was looking for something that couldn't be found.
Then Dave called.

"Golf, mate. Saturday morning. You in?"

Norman had played golf exactly three times in his life, all of them work outings where he'd been too anxious about his swing to enjoy the walk. But Dave was persistent, and the condo was quiet, and the loneliness was loud.

"Sure," Norman said. "I know someone. An umbrella girl. She can be our caddie."

He texted Lilette. She responded within minutes. Yes, she was available. Yes, she would be happy to see him. Yes, she remembered their dinner.

The golf course was green and beautiful and utterly indifferent to the chaos of the city below. Mountains rose in the distance, hazy and blue. The air was cooler up here, cleaner, scented with cut grass and something floral Norman couldn't name. Dave was in high spirits, talking trash about his handicap, his swing, his chances of beating Norman despite Norman's obvious lack of skill.

Lilette met them at the clubhouse. She wore her uniform—the bright polo, the visor, the smile—and she greeted Norman with a warmth that felt genuine, or at

least professionally convincing. He introduced her to Dave, who lit up like a Christmas tree.
"Lovely to meet you, Lilette. Norman's told me all about you."

He hadn't, but Dave was a salesman by nature and by trade. Norman watched as Dave maneuvered closer to her on the first tee, asking questions about the course, the best lines, the local knowledge. Norman hung back, content to be the third wheel, to watch the possibility of connection happen to someone else.

On the third hole, as Dave lined up a putt, Norman pulled Lilette aside.

"My friend likes you," he said quietly. "Dave. He's a good guy. Retired, got his finances in order, looking for someone to share his life with. You should give him a chance."

Lilette looked at him. Her expression didn't change, but something shifted behind her eyes. That distance he'd noticed at dinner, the wall he couldn't see—it seemed to lower, just slightly.
"I like you better," she said.

The words were simple. Direct. They landed in Norman's chest like a stone dropped in still water. He was fifty-eight years old. He had been overlooked, underestimated, rejected, and betrayed by life and love and the country of his birth. He had come to the other side of the world to escape, to hide, to build something new from the ruins of his old self. And here was this woman, twenty-three years old, beautiful in her boyish way, telling him that she chose him. Not Dave with his Australian confidence and his retirement fund. Him. Norman. The quiet one. The one who always expected to be passed over.

He didn't know what to say. So he said nothing. He just nodded, and they finished the round in a silence that felt different from the silence of the rice field. This silence was charged, electric, full of words unspoken and possibilities unexplored.

Dave, oblivious, talked through the remaining holes. He talked about his swing, his ex-wife, his plans to buy a boat. Norman nodded at the right moments, laughed at the right jokes, but his mind was elsewhere. It was with the umbrella girl, walking beside him, her visor shading her eyes, her secret tucked away like a small, dangerous gift.

At the end of the round, Dave shook her hand warmly and told her she was the best caddie he'd ever had. Norman walked her back to the caddie shack.

"Dinner again?" he asked. "This week?"

She smiled, and this time the smile reached her eyes. "Yes. I would like that."

He watched her walk away, her short hair catching the sunlight, her figure small against the vast green of the course. The low-grade fever in his bones had changed. It was no longer just the weight of history, the sediment of 347 years. It was something else now. Something warmer. Something more dangerous.

Hope.

End-of-Chapter Question: Is love at first sight a myth, or is it the quiet, desperate hope for connection that makes us see what we want to see?

Chapter 7: The Proposal and the Mother's Teeth

The second dinner was longer than the first. The third was longer still. By the fourth, Norman had stopped counting and started believing.

Lilette was unlike anyone he had met in the parade. She asked questions that went beyond the surface—not about his money or his condo or his American passport, but about his childhood, his father, the books he read, the music he loved. She listened to his answers with an intensity that made him feel, for the first time in years, that he was being seen. Not as a rich foreigner, not as a potential ticket to a better life, but as a man. A complicated, wounded, hopeful man.

But there were moments. Small things. The way her mood could shift in an instant—warm and present one minute, distant and cool the next. The way she sometimes seemed to forget things they had discussed, details he was certain they had shared. The way her eyes would go flat, just for a moment, like a light switched off behind them.

Norman noticed these things. He was not a fool. But he was a lonely man, and loneliness has a way of explaining away the unexplained. She's tired, he told himself. She's under stress. She has family problems she doesn't want to burden me with. He made excuses for her because he wanted to, because the alternative was too painful to consider.

Three weeks after the golf game, she said the words that changed everything.

They were sitting on his balcony, watching the city lights blur and shimmer below them. The air was warm, thick with the smell of the sea and the distant noise of traffic. She had been quiet for a long time, her head resting against his shoulder, her short hair soft against his cheek. Then she lifted her head and looked at him, and her eyes were different—softer, younger somehow, full of a vulnerability he hadn't seen before.
"I want to marry you," she said.

Norman's heart stopped. Then started again, faster.

"What?"

"I want to be your wife. I want to have your children. I want to build a life with you."

The words hung in the air between them, simple and enormous. Norman thought of all the reasons this was insane. The age difference. The short time they had known each other. The mood swings he couldn't explain, the distance that came and went like weather. He thought of Rosalie, the quiet one who had stolen from him. He thought of his father, warning him about the world, about people, about the dangers of trusting too fast.

But he also thought of the loneliness. The golden jail. The long nights in his huge bed with no one to hold. He thought of his mother, dead now twenty years, who had told him on her deathbed to find someone, to not die alone, to let himself be loved.

"Yes," he said.

The word came out before he could stop it, before he could examine it, before he could weigh it against all the sensible objections. It came from somewhere deeper than sense, somewhere more desperate. It came from the part of him that had been waiting his whole life to be chosen.

Lilette smiled. She kissed him, softly, and then she rested her head against his shoulder again, and they watched the city lights in silence. Norman felt something he hadn't felt in decades. Peace. Or the illusion of peace. At this point, he couldn't tell the difference.

The engagement was a secret at first, just theirs. But Lilette wanted to tell her family. She wanted her mother's blessing. She wanted Norman to meet her properly, not just the quick hello at the beginning of a date, but a real meeting, a family dinner, a chance for her mother to see the man she had chosen.

Norman agreed, though something in him stirred uneasily. He remembered the mood swings, the forgotten conversations, the way Lilette sometimes looked at him like a stranger. He pushed the thoughts away. He was engaged. He was happy. He would meet her mother, and everything would be fine.

The mother lived in a barangay on the edge of the city, a place of narrow streets and small houses pressed together like books on a shelf. Lilette guided him through the maze, past children playing with tires and dogs sleeping in the shade, to a small concrete house with a corrugated tin roof and a single flowering plant in a rusted can by the door.

The woman who opened the door was not what Norman expected.

She was thin, painfully thin, with hollow cheeks and eyes that seemed too large for her face. Her skin had the grayish pallor of someone who hadn't seen the sun in months, or who had seen too much of something else. Her hair was thin, pulled back tightly, revealing a high forehead and a nervous tic that made her blink too fast. And her teeth. Norman couldn't stop looking at her teeth. They were brown, rotting, some missing entirely, the remnants of what must have once been a smile now a ruin.

He knew those teeth. He had seen them before, in the faces of addicts on Chicago streets, in the mugshots of men destroyed by crack, in the hollow eyes of Rosalie before he fired her. Shabu. The local meth. The drug that had eaten through his petty cash and his trust.

"Mom, this is Norman," Lilette said, her voice bright, cheerful, as if she didn't see what Norman saw. "Norman, this is my mother, Aling Belen."

The mother smiled, revealing the ruin of her mouth, and extended a hand that trembled slightly. Norman took it. Her grip was weak, her skin dry and cool.

"Welcome," she said, her voice a whisper. "Welcome to our home."

They sat on plastic chairs in a small living room decorated with religious images and family photographs. The mother asked polite questions—where was he from, what did he do, how did he meet her daughter—and Norman answered, but his mind was elsewhere. He was watching her hands, the way they shook. He was watching her eyes, the way they darted to Lilette for cues. He was watching her teeth, the undeniable evidence of a poison he knew too well.

Lilette's father, she had said, was in jail. For drugs. But looking at the mother, Norman wondered if the wrong parent was behind bars.

Later, after the mother had retired to a back room, claiming tiredness, Norman and Lilette sat outside on a low wall, watching children chase each other in the fading light.

"Your mother," Norman said carefully. "Is she okay? She seems... unwell."

Lilette's face closed for a moment. That flatness he had seen before, the light behind her eyes switching off. Then it passed, and she smiled.

"She's fine," she said. "Just tired. She works very hard."

Norman wanted to push. He wanted to ask about the teeth, the tremors, the unmistakable signs of addiction. But he didn't know how. He didn't know if he had the right. He didn't know if asking would shatter something fragile, something he was only beginning to build.

"My father," Lilette said quietly, as if reading his thoughts, "he is the one with problems. Drugs. That's why he's in jail. My mother, she is clean. She has been clean for years. I promise you."

She looked at him, her eyes wide and earnest. Norman wanted to believe her. He needed to believe her. Because if he couldn't believe her, what was left? Another betrayal.

Another Rosalie. Another proof that the world was exactly what his father had warned him it was.

He nodded. "Okay. I believe you."

The lie tasted like nothing. Like the air. Like the low-grade fever he had carried his whole life.

That night, alone in his condo, Norman stood at the window and looked out at the city. He was engaged to be married. He was going to be a husband, maybe a father. He had found someone who chose him, who wanted him, who promised him a future.
But the image of the mother's teeth lingered. Rotting. Accusing. A warning he couldn't unsee.

And beneath that image, something else. A memory of Lilette's face when he had asked about her mother. That flatness. That stranger looking out through her eyes. He had seen it before, many times, and he had always explained it away. But now, for the first time, he wondered if there was something to explain. Something he couldn't see. Something hidden in the spaces between her moods, waiting to be found.

End-of-Chapter Question: When the woman you love tells you a story that doesn't quite add up, do you listen to your gut or your heart?

Chapter 8: The Vanishing and the Twin

The mountainside home was a dream made of concrete and glass.

Norman found it through a realtor recommended by Dave, a sharp-faced woman named Mrs. Chua who spoke with the efficient authority of someone who had never been denied anything. The property sat on a ridge overlooking a valley of green, the city a distant glitter on the horizon, the air cool and clean and scented with pine. It was still under construction, a frame of steel and raw concrete, but Norman could see what it would become. Floor-to-ceiling windows. An infinity pool that would seem to spill into the sky. A master bedroom larger than his entire Chicago apartment.

Lilette's eyes went wide when she saw it. She walked through the empty rooms, her footsteps echoing on the concrete, her hand trailing along walls that would soon be painted and perfect. She talked about where the furniture would go, where the children would play, where they would sit and watch the sunset. Norman watched her talk and felt something expand in his chest. This was what it meant to build a future. This was what it meant to have someone to build it for.

Mrs. Chua handled the negotiations. The owner was a Chinese-Filipino businessman who lived in Manila, who wanted to unload the property quickly, who was willing to accept a reasonable offer. Norman made the offer. The owner accepted. Papers were drawn up. A down payment was required, a substantial sum, to secure the property while the legal details were finalized.

Lilette volunteered to handle it.

"I know people," she said. "I can help with the paperwork, the translations, the bank transfers. You don't need to worry about any of it. Just focus on your business. Let me take care of this for us."

Norman hesitated. The sum was significant, even for him. And there was something in her eagerness that gave him pause, a flicker of the old caution, the voice of his father whispering warnings. But he looked at her face, so bright with hope, so eager to contribute, to be his partner, to build their future together. He remembered the mother's teeth, the father in jail, the gaps in her story that he had chosen not to question. He remembered Rosalie, the quiet one, the trustworthy one, the thief.
But this was different. This was Lilette. This was love.

He transferred the money.

The days that followed were busy. Norman had clients to serve, projects to manage, a business to run. Lilette handled the house details, or said she did. She reported progress—the papers were moving through channels, the owner was cooperative, there were minor delays but nothing to worry about. Norman trusted her. He had to.

Then the calls stopped.

Not completely, at first. Just a slower response here, a missed call there. Then longer silences. Then excuses—phone problems, family emergencies, a sick relative who needed her attention. Norman's caution, never fully asleep, began to stir.

He called Mrs. Chua.

"The mountainside property," he said. "Can you give me an update on the paperwork?"

A pause. "Mr. Wright, I assumed you had withdrawn your offer. The owner said his representative informed him you were no longer interested."

The words landed like stones. "His representative?"

"Your fiancée, I believe. She contacted him directly, said you had changed your mind, and arranged for the down payment to be returned. To her, I assume, since she was your authorized representative. I'm sorry, I thought you knew."

Norman hung up. He sat at his desk, the city humming outside his window, and felt the world tilt slightly on its axis. The down payment. The money. The woman he loved.

He called Lilette. No answer. He called again. Nothing. He texted, messaged, emailed. The silence was absolute, a wall where her voice used to be.
Three days passed. Norman barely ate, barely slept. He ran through scenarios in his mind—a mistake, a misunderstanding, a problem she was trying to solve on her own. He clung to each possibility like a drowning man, but the current was strong and the shore was far away.

On the fourth day, she called.

"Norman, I'm so sorry. My phone broke. My mother got sick. Everything has been chaos. I'm coming to see you tonight. We need to talk."

Relief flooded through him, warm and immediate. He wanted to believe. He needed to believe. He told himself the story he needed to hear—mistakes, not malice; chaos, not conspiracy.

That evening, he waited at a café near his condo, watching the door, rehearsing what he would say. He would be understanding. He would be kind. He would give her the chance to explain.

She walked in, and his heart lifted. Same short hair. Same smile. Same walk. She slid into the seat across from him, reached for his hand, and began to apologize. The words washed over him—phone problems, sick mother, so sorry, still love you, still want to marry you, please understand.

Norman listened. He nodded. He squeezed her hand. And something in the back of his mind, some small, quiet part of him, noticed something off. A gesture. A phrase. The way she tilted her head.

But he pushed it away. He was too relieved to question. Too desperate to doubt.

They talked for an hour. She promised to fix things with the house, to get the money back, to make everything right. He believed her. He had to.

The next morning, he went to the market near her barangay. He didn't know why. Some instinct, some buried suspicion, some need to see her world, to understand the gaps in her story. He walked through the crowded aisles, past vendors selling fish and vegetables and knockoff perfumes, and then he saw her.

Lilette. Standing at a fruit stall, examining mangoes.

He started towards her, a smile forming on his face. Then he stopped.

There was something wrong. The way she stood. The clothes she wore. The expression on her face as she haggled with the vendor—a hardness he had never seen, a sharpness that didn't belong to the woman who held his hand and promised him a future.

He called her name.

She looked up. Their eyes met. And in that moment, Norman knew.

This was not Lilette.

The face was the same. The body was the same. But the eyes were different. They looked at him without recognition, without warmth, without the love he had convinced himself was real. They looked at him the way you look at a stranger who has called you by the wrong name.

"Who are you?" he asked.

The woman tilted her head, a gesture that was familiar and utterly alien. Then she smiled, a smile that was nothing like Lilette's.

"I'm sorry," she said. "You must be mistaking me for someone else."

She turned and walked away, disappearing into the crowd. Norman stood frozen, the market noise washing over him, the smell of fish and fruit and exhaust filling his lungs. He didn't move for a long time.

That night, he confronted Lilette. She came to his condo, her face arranged in concern, asking what was wrong, why did he sound so strange on the phone. He told her what he saw. The market. The woman. The face that was hers and not hers.

Lilette listened. Her expression shifted—surprise, then understanding, then something else, something he couldn't name.

"That was my twin," she said quietly.

The words hung in the air. Twin. The sister mentioned once and never again. The gap in her story, now filled with a living, breathing person.

"I didn't tell you because I didn't want to confuse you," Lilette said. "We are close. Very close. Sometimes people mistake us. It happens. I'm sorry you had to find out like this."

Norman wanted to ask more. He wanted to know why the secret, why the silence, why the woman at the market had looked at him like a stranger when she must have known exactly who he was. But the questions tangled in his throat, and Lilette was holding his hand, and her eyes were so earnest, so convincing, so much like the woman he loved.

He let it go. He told himself it didn't matter. He told himself the twin was just a detail, a quirk of family, nothing to fear.

But that night, alone in his bed, he couldn't sleep. He kept seeing the woman at the market. The stranger in Lilette's face. The door that had swung shut on a trap he was only beginning to understand.

He thought of his father then, for the first time in weeks. Heard his voice, low and rough, warning him about the world. They ain't looking for a reason, son. They're looking for an excuse.

But what were they looking for here? What excuse? What reason?

He didn't know. He only knew that something had shifted, some foundation had cracked, and he would never again look at Lilette without wondering which sister he was seeing.

End-of-Chapter Question: If you can no longer trust that the person you love is one single person, what is left to hold onto?

Chapter 9: The Nostalgia Trap

The twin haunted him.

Not in dreams, not in shadows, but in the small spaces between moments—the pause before Lilette answered a question, the turn of her head when she thought he wasn't watching, the way her voice sometimes shifted into registers he didn't recognize. Norman found himself studying her now, watching for the flicker of difference, the tell that would reveal which sister sat across from him at dinner, which sister held his hand, which sister promised to love him forever.

He never caught her. Or maybe he did, and convinced himself he hadn't. The mind was a strange thing, capable of holding two truths at once—the truth of what you see and the truth of what you need to believe.

Lilette, or the woman who called herself Lilette, seemed untroubled by his scrutiny. She moved through their life with the same warmth, the same affection, the same occasional distance that he had come to accept as part of who she was. She talked about the mountainside house, the lost down payment, the complications with the owner. She promised to make it right, to find a way, to never let him down again.

Norman let her talk. He listened. He nodded. But something in him had shifted, a gear that could not be unshifted. The trust was cracked, and cracks, once made, do not heal.

He needed an anchor. Something solid. Something real.

The island friends became that anchor.

He had met them months ago, before Lilette, before the engagement, before the twin revelation. A couple—Benjie and Cora—who ran a small resort on a nearby island, a place of white sand and turquoise water and simple cottages built from bamboo and coconut wood. They were from Manila originally, educated, well-traveled, who had traded city stress for island peace. They welcomed Norman like family, fed him grilled fish and fresh mangoes, listened to his stories and told their own.

When the cracks in his life with Lilette began to show, Norman retreated to them. Weekends on the island. Long talks on the beach. The simple comfort of people who wanted nothing from him but his company.

Benjie was the first to notice the change.

"You seem different, man. Heavier. Something wrong?"

They sat on the resort's deck, watching the sun melt into the sea. Norman considered lying, then let the truth spill out—the twin, the money, the mountainside house, the creeping sense that he was caught in something he didn't understand.

Benjie listened without interrupting. When Norman finished, he was quiet for a long time.

"Be careful," he said finally. "Family here, it's different. The bonds are strong. Sometimes too strong. Sometimes people get caught up in things bigger than themselves."

Norman wanted to ask what he meant, but Benjie stood, stretched, and said something about checking on dinner. The moment passed.

Cora was more direct.

"She's using you," she said one afternoon, as they walked along the beach. "I'm sorry to say it, but someone has to. I see the way she looks at you. Not like a woman looks at a man she loves. Like a woman looks at a solution to a problem."

Norman bristled, defended, protested. But the words lodged in him anyway, small seeds of doubt planted in already cracked soil.

He stopped going to the island. Not because he was angry, but because he was afraid they were right.

The proposal came from Lilette's family.
Not Lilette herself, but her mother—the hollow-cheeked woman with the ruined teeth—and a woman she introduced as her sister, though Norman had learned by now that "sister" could mean anything. They came to his condo one evening, unannounced, bearing food and smiles and an offer they said would change his life.

"There is a rice farm," the mother said, her voice a thin whisper. "In the province. Our province. Where we come from. It is for sale. Good land, good water, good people. You could buy it. Build something. Be a farmer, like you always wanted."

Norman stared at her. "Like I always wanted?"

Lilette, sitting beside him, squeezed his hand. "I told them about your first days here. About the rice farmer who took you in. About how happy you were in the province. I told them it was your fondest memory."

The words landed like a blow to the chest. His fondest memory. The rice field under moonlight. The simple kindness of strangers. Maria's smile, unburdened by wanting. He had shared these things with Lilette in the early days, in the falling days, when he was still trying to make her understand who he was and where he came from. He had given her his most precious memories, the only pure things he had found in this country, and now she was handing them back to him, wrapped in an offer he couldn't refuse.

The farm. A rice farm of his own. The chance to live the dream that had haunted him since his first night in the province. To be not just a rich foreigner in a glass tower, but a man connected to the land, to the rhythm of planting and harvest, to the simple dignity of feeding people.

He looked at Lilette. She smiled. He looked at the mother. She smiled too, a ghastly thing with her ruined teeth. He looked at the sister, who smiled last and longest.

"Yes," he said. "Tell me more."

The negotiations were swift. The farm was in the north, in the same region where Norman had spent his first weeks. The price was fair, they said. The owner was motivated. The papers could be signed quickly. Norman visited once, a flying visit arranged by the family, and saw the land—green and flat and bordered by a river, with a small house that could be expanded, a view of distant hills that made his heart ache with memory.

He bought it.

Then he built on it.

The mansion rose from the rice fields like a dream of wealth in a world of poverty. Marble floors and high ceilings and windows that caught the morning light. It stood next to the simple farmhouse where the workers lived, a monument to the contradiction at the heart of his life—the man who wanted peace and the man who could only buy it.

He built piggeries too, long concrete structures where hundreds of pigs would be fattened for market. He bought cattle, cows and bulls that grazed in pastures that had been rice fields. He gave money to the village—built an elementary school stadium where children could play, a community center where families could gather, a park with benches and flowering trees. He paved roads that had been mud for generations. He gave millions to the poor, to families who came to his gate with stories of sickness and hardship and need.

The community loved him. They called him "Sir Norman" with reverence, invited him to fiestas, named their children after him. He walked through the village and saw smiles everywhere, felt the warmth of gratitude like sunlight on his skin.

And all the while, Lilette and her family were there. Managing things. Handling money. Making decisions. They were indispensable, they said. They were family, they said. They were looking out for his interests, they said.

The island friends came to visit once, to see what he had built. Benjie walked through the mansion in silence, his face unreadable. Cora sat with Norman on his veranda, looking out at the rice fields.

"It's beautiful," she said. "What you've done here."

Norman nodded, proud.

"But I still worry about you," she added. "All these people, all this need. It's a lot of weight for one man to carry."

"I'm not carrying it alone," Norman said. "I have Lilette. I have her family."

Cora looked at him. Her eyes were sad. "That's what worries me."

They left the next day. Norman watched their boat disappear down the river and felt a pang of something— loss, maybe, or loneliness, or the first faint stirring of a fear he had been refusing to name.

He turned back to his mansion, his farm, his pigs, his cattle, his roads, his school, his park, his community. His family. His Lilette. His dream, built on the foundation of his fondest memory.

That night, he dreamed of Maria. She stood in the rice field under moonlight, her bare feet in the water, her smile gentle and sad. She didn't speak. She didn't need to. Her eyes said everything.

You gave them your memories, those eyes said. And they used them to build your cage.

He woke in the dark, the image fading, the feeling lingering. The low-grade fever in his bones had changed again. It was no longer the weight of history, the sediment of 347 years. It was no longer the warmth of hope, the danger of love. It was something else now. Something colder. Something that felt like the beginning of knowing.

He lay in the dark and listened to the sounds of his kingdom—the distant grunt of pigs, the lowing of cattle, the whisper of wind through the rice. And somewhere, in the rooms below, the soft footsteps of the family who had given him everything and taken everything in return. The nostalgia trap. The most beautiful cage of all.

End-of-Chapter Question: Can a memory be so powerful that it becomes a weapon used against you, blinding you to the enemy standing right in front of you?

Chapter 10: The Society of Women

The truth did not arrive like a thunderbolt. It arrived like dawn—slow, gradual, unavoidable.

Norman had built his kingdom in the rice fields. The mansion stood gleaming against the green, a monument to his success, his generosity, his dream made concrete. The villagers called him "Sir Norman" with genuine affection. Children played in the school stadium he had built. Families gathered in the community center he had funded. Old women sat on the benches in his park, watching their grandchildren chase each other through the flowering trees.

He was loved. He was respected. He was, for the first time in his life, exactly where he belonged.

And yet.

The cracks he had ignored for so long were widening. Small things, at first. A neighbor's comment, meant to be helpful, that lingered in his mind longer than it should. A look exchanged between Lilette and her mother, too quick to read, too knowing to ignore. The way the twin—whom he had still not officially met, though he saw her sometimes in the village, always at a distance—seemed to appear and disappear like a ghost.

The first real crack came from a woman in the village. An old woman, Lola Puring, who had lived in the province her whole life and had seen things, she said, that would make a young man's blood run cold. Norman had given her money for medicine, for her grandchildren, for the roof that leaked when it rained. She was grateful, fiercely loyal, and she watched everything.

One afternoon, she appeared at his gate. Norman invited her in, offered her food, drink, a seat in the shade. She accepted the seat but refused the rest. Her eyes, clouded with age but sharp with intent, fixed on his face.

"Sir Norman," she said quietly, "you are a good man. Too good for this place, maybe. But you are here, and so I must tell you what I see."

Norman waited.

"That family," she said. "The one you tied yourself to. I knew them when they were children. I knew their mother before she lost herself to the drugs. I knew their grandmother, who was a hard woman, a woman who hated men with a hate that burned like fire. She passed it to her daughter. And the daughter passed it to her girls."

Norman's chest tightened. "What are you saying?"

"I am saying that those girls were raised to see men as enemies. As things to be used and discarded. Their grandmother was beaten by her husband, a cruel man who drank and gambled and left her with nothing. Their mother was beaten by hers, the same story, the same pain. They learned young that men bring nothing but suffering. So they learned to take instead. To take everything and give nothing back."

The old woman leaned closer. Her breath was warm, her voice a whisper.

"They are not lovers of men, Sir Norman. They are lovers of each other. The twins, they are close in ways that sisters should not be. And their mother protects them, enables them, helps them. They have others too, women who come and go, who live not far from your farm. It is a society of women, bound together by blood and by hate. And you, Sir Norman, are their project."

Norman sat perfectly still. The words should have shocked him. They should have landed like blows, like the betrayal he had always feared. But instead, they landed like answers. Like pieces of a puzzle he had been staring at for months, finally clicking into place.

The twin. The switching. The way Lilette sometimes seemed to forget things they had discussed, places they had been, words they had shared. The mother's complicity, her knowing looks, her careful management of every interaction. The father in jail—conveniently absent, conveniently blamed for all the family's problems.

The girlfriends nearby, always mentioned but never introduced.

A society of women. Bound by blood and hate. Using him.

He thanked Lola Puring. He walked her to the gate, watched her slow progress down the dirt road, her small figure growing smaller until it disappeared into the haze of afternoon heat. Then he went back inside and sat in his beautiful living room, surrounded by his beautiful things, and waited.

For what, he did not know.

Lilette came that evening, as she always did. She brought food—his favorite dishes, the ones she knew he loved. She set the table. She smiled. She was the picture of the devoted fiancée, the future wife, the partner in his dream.

Norman watched her move through his house and saw her differently. Not as the woman he loved, but as a stranger performing a role. Every gesture, every smile, every word was a line from a script written long before he arrived. He was not her lover. He was her mark.

After dinner, they sat on the veranda. The rice fields stretched before them, silver under the rising moon. The same moon that had welcomed him his first night in the province. The same fields that had filled him with peace.

"We need to talk," Norman said.

Lilette turned to him, her face soft, questioning. The face of the woman he had fallen for. The face of the woman who had promised to love him forever.

"Tell me about your grandmother," he said.

A flicker. So quick he almost missed it. Then the mask was back.

"My grandmother? She died when I was young. I barely remember her."

"Tell me what you remember."

A pause. The first real pause. The first crack in the performance.

"She was... strict. Hard. She didn't smile much. My mother said she had a difficult life."

"Did she hate men?"

The question hung in the air between them. Lilette's face did not change, but something behind her eyes shifted. A door opening. A door closing. A decision being made.

"Why would you ask that?"

"Someone told me something today. About your family. About how the women in your family see men. About what you were raised to be."

Lilette was silent for a long moment. The night insects sang their endless song. A dog barked in the distance. The moon climbed higher, indifferent to the small human drama unfolding beneath it.

Then she laughed.

It was not the bell-like sound he remembered from their early days. It was something else—hard, bitter, old. A sound that had nothing to do with joy and everything to do with survival.

"You finally figured it out," she said. "I wondered how long it would take. You're smarter than most, I'll give you that. Most of them never figure it out. They just keep giving until there's nothing left to give."

Norman looked at her. This woman he had loved. This woman he had trusted. This woman he had built a kingdom for.

"It was all a lie?"

"All of it." Her voice was flat now, empty. "The love. The dreams. The talk of marriage and children. Every word. Every smile. Every time I held your hand and looked into your eyes like you were the only man in the world. All of it was a performance."

"Why?"

She turned to face him fully. In the moonlight, her face was beautiful and terrible, a mask stripped of all pretense.

"Because men took everything from my grandmother. Everything from my mother. They used them and threw them away like garbage. My grandmother's husband beat her until she couldn't walk, then left her with nothing but children and debt. My mother's husband did the same, then found God in prison and left her to rot. Men don't love us, Norman. They use us. So we learned to use them first."

"You could have chosen differently."

"Chosen differently?" She laughed again, that same bitter sound. "You think we had a choice? You think any of this was a choice? This is survival. This is what we were taught, what we had to learn, what we became to stay alive. You came here with your money and your loneliness and your desperate need to be loved. You were perfect. Easy. A gift from the gods."

Norman thought of all the moments he had treasured. The dinners, the conversations, the quiet evenings on this very veranda. All of them lies. All of them performances. All of them nothing.

"The twin," he said. "She was in on it too."

"Of course. We all were. My mother. My sister. Our friends. We are a family, Norman. A real family. We take care of each other. And you—you were just a way to do that."

"The mountainside house. The down payment."

"Gone. Spent. Shared. You'll never see it again."

"The farm. The mansion. Everything I built."

"Built on our land, with our help, through our connections. The people here love us. They've known us forever. You're just the foreigner who paid for everything. Without us, you're nothing here. Less than nothing."

Norman stood. He walked to the edge of the veranda and looked out at the rice fields. They were beautiful. They were peaceful. They were his, and they were not his. Everything he had built, everything he had loved, everything he had believed—all of it rested on a foundation of lies.

"Get out," he said quietly.

Lilette stood. She walked to the door, then paused. In the doorway, backlit by the light from inside, she looked like a ghost. Like something that had never been real.

"You'll stay, though," she said. "You'll stay because you built this. Because you love this place. Because you have nowhere else to go. And we'll be here, Norman. Waiting. Always waiting. Because this is our home. Our province. Our country. And you—you're just a visitor. A very rich, very stupid visitor who thought he could buy his way into a family."

She left. The door closed softly behind her.

Norman stood alone on the veranda, looking out at the fields. The moon was high now, painting the world in silver and shadow. Somewhere in the village, a dog barked. Somewhere in the darkness, a family of women was celebrating another victory, another mark drained, another man destroyed.

He thought of his father. He thought of the traffic stop, the job interviews, the long years of being told he was too much and not enough. He thought of the plane ride here, the hope that had bloomed in his chest when he stepped off that plane. He thought of Maria, the translator, the only one who had seen him clearly, the only one who had given him something real.

He had left her behind. He had chosen this instead.

The low-grade fever in his bones was gone now, replaced by something colder. Something that felt like truth. He had fled America to escape one kind of prison, only to build another with his own hands. He had given his trust, his money, his heart to people who saw him as nothing but a resource to be mined. He had been fooled, scammed, used—not just by one woman, but by a family, a society, a generations-old machine of vengeance and greed.

The romance was a lie. The proposal was a con. The future he had imagined was a fiction written by strangers who hated him for reasons that had nothing to do with him.

He was alone. Really alone. For the first time since arriving in this country, he understood what that meant.

But he was still here. Still standing. Still breathing.

And somewhere in the darkness, they were waiting.

End-of-Chapter Question: When you realize the love story of your life was actually a horror story, do you mourn the love you lost, or the person you became for it?

Chapter 11: A Taste of Paradise

The days after the confrontation were strange, hollow things.

Norman moved through his kingdom like a ghost in his own story. He walked the rice fields at dawn, watching the farmers bend over their work, their backs curved like question marks against the rising sun. He visited his piggeries, his cattle, his school, his park. He sat on his veranda and watched the light change over the mountains, gold to green to purple to black. He was everywhere and nowhere, present and absent, a man going through the motions of a life that no longer felt like his own.

The village continued around him, indifferent to his private apocalypse. Children still played in the school stadium. Families still gathered in the community center. Old women still sat on the benches in his park, watching their grandchildren chase each other through the flowering trees. They greeted him warmly—"Good morning, Sir Norman!"—and he smiled and waved and felt nothing at all.

Lilette did not come to the house. Neither did her mother, her twin, any of the women who had populated his life for the past year. They were waiting, as she had said. Waiting for him to make a move, to decide, to do something they could predict and exploit.

He did nothing.
What was there to do? Confront them again? The truth was already told. Call the police? For what? A down payment he had willingly transferred? A lie he had willingly believed? In this country, in this province, in this village, they were family and he was the foreigner. The police would listen, nod, and do nothing. He knew this the way he knew the sun would rise, the way he knew the rice would grow, the way he knew the low-grade fever of his history would never fully leave his bones.

So he waited. For what, he did not know.

The invitation came on a Thursday.

A girl from the village—one of the many children who ran through his park—appeared at his gate with a folded piece of paper. Norman took it, unfolded it, read the words written in careful, schoolgirl English.

Dear Sir Norman,
Please come to dinner at our house on Saturday. We want to talk. We want to explain. We want to make things right.
Your family,
Lilette

His family. The word was a knife, but he read it again anyway. We want to explain. We want to make things right. He knew it was probably a lie. He knew they probably wanted something—more money, more access, more opportunities to drain him dry. He knew he should throw the note away, ignore it, pretend he had never received it.

But he also knew he could not.

Because some part of him, some stupid, hopeful, desperate part, still wanted to believe. Still wanted the story to have a different ending. Still wanted the woman he loved to be real.

Saturday came.

Norman dressed carefully—simple clothes, nothing that suggested wealth or status. He walked to their house, the same small concrete structure in the same narrow barangay where he had first met the mother with the ruined teeth. The walk took forty minutes. He used every one of them to tell himself to turn back, to go home, to protect what little was left of his heart.

He did not turn back.

The mother opened the door. She looked the same—thin, hollow, her teeth a ruin, her eyes too large for her face. But there was something different in those eyes tonight. Something softer. Something almost like welcome.

"Sir Norman," she said. "Come in. Please. We have been waiting."

He stepped inside.

The house was small but clean. Religious images on the walls. Plastic covers on the furniture. The smell of cooking—his favorite dishes, the ones he had bragged about, the ones Lilette had learned to make perfectly. His stomach turned at the smell, but he sat where they indicated, accepted the drink they offered, waited for whatever came next.

They came one by one.

The mother first, settling into a chair across from him, her hands folded in her lap, her eyes watching him with an intensity that made his skin crawl.

Then the twin.

She entered from a back room, and for a moment Norman's heart stopped. She looked exactly like Lilette—the same face, the same body, the same short hair. But her eyes were different. Harder. Older. She sat beside the mother and looked at Norman with an expression he could not read.

Then Lilette.
She came last, through the same door, and took a seat on his other side. Now he was surrounded. Three women, three faces, two of them identical, all of them watching him like he was something fragile, something precious, something they were afraid might break.

"We wanted to explain," Lilette said quietly. "Really explain. Not the lies. The truth."

Norman said nothing.

"Our grandmother," the mother began, her thin voice filling the small room. "She was fifteen when she was married. Fifteen. To a man twice her age. He beat her. He gambled away everything they had. He left her with three children and a debt that took twenty years to pay. She died at fifty, but she looked eighty. That is what men did to her."

She paused, looked at her daughters, then back at Norman.

"I was seventeen when I married. I thought I knew better. I thought I had chosen differently. But my husband was the same man in a different skin. He drank. He used drugs. He hit me when I complained, hit me when I didn't, hit me because hitting was what men did. He is in jail now, and I thank God every day that he is there, because if he were here, I would not be alive."

The twin spoke next. Her voice was lower than Lilette's, rougher, as if it had been used for different purposes.

"We grew up watching this. Watching our mother bleed, watching our grandmother die, watching men destroy the women we loved. We learned early that men were not to be trusted. That men were not to be loved. That men were things to be used before they could use you."

Lilette reached for Norman's hand. He let her take it, but he did not squeeze back.

"We know what we did was wrong," she said. "We know we hurt you. We know we lied and cheated and stole. But we want you to understand why. Not to excuse it. Just to understand."

Norman looked at them. Three generations of women, bound by blood and pain and a hatred that had been passed down like an inheritance. He thought of his own history—the 347 years, the Jim Crow, the traffic stops, the job interviews, the slow poison of a thousand small humiliations. He knew what it was to be shaped by suffering. He knew what it was to carry the weight of generations.

But he also knew that suffering did not excuse cruelty. That pain did not justify theft. That being hurt did not give you the right to hurt others.

"I understand," he said quietly. "But understanding is not the same as forgiving."

The mother nodded slowly. "We know. We do not ask for forgiveness. Not yet. We ask only for a chance. A chance to show you that we can be different. That we want to be different."

The twin looked at him, and for the first time, her eyes softened. "You are the first man who has ever treated us like people. Like we mattered. Like we were more than just bodies or opportunities. That means something. It means more than you know."

Lilette squeezed his hand. "Stay for dinner. Please. Let us feed you. Let us show you that we can give something back. Even if it's just a meal."

Norman looked at the food on the table. His favorite dishes. Prepared with care. The smell was intoxicating, familiar, comforting. He thought of all the meals they had shared, all the evenings he had sat across from Lilette and felt, for the first time in his life, that he belonged somewhere.

He was hungry. He was tired. He was lonely.

He stayed.

The food was delicious.

Everything he had bragged about, everything he had missed from his mother's kitchen, everything he had taught Lilette to make—it was all there, perfect, beautiful, a feast of memory and comfort. He ate slowly at first, then faster, the flavors flooding his mouth, warming his chest, filling the empty spaces inside him.

They talked as he ate. Not about the past, not about the lies, but about small things. The village. The farm. The children in the park. The weather. Safe things. Easy things. Things that could be shared without pain.

Norman relaxed. The food was good. The company was almost warm. The women laughed at his stories, asked questions about his childhood, listened with what seemed like genuine interest. For a moment—just a moment—he allowed himself to pretend that things could be different. That the past could be rewritten. That love could still be possible.

Then the warmth in his chest changed.

It spread slowly at first, a gentle heat that felt like contentment. Then it deepened, sharpened, became something else. Something heavy. Something wrong.

Norman set down his fork. He looked at the women. They were watching him, all three of them, their faces perfectly still. Waiting.

"What—" he started, but the word was thick, clumsy, wrong in his mouth.

The room seemed to darken at the edges. The sounds of the village—distant dogs, children playing, the endless hum of life—faded into a muffled silence. His heart was beating too fast, then too slow, then somewhere in between.

He tried to stand. His legs would not obey. They were heavy, useless, made of something that was not bone and muscle.

Lilette was looking at him. Her face was soft, almost sad. The twin's face was harder, watching like a scientist observing an experiment. The mother's face was blank, empty of everything except waiting.

"Why?" Norman managed. The word was a whisper, a breath, almost nothing.

No one answered.

The room was dimming now, the edges dissolving into shadow. He could still see them—three women, three faces, two of them identical—sitting perfectly still, watching him die.

He thought of the rice field. His first night in the province. The silver stalks under the moonlight. The farmer's silent welcome. Maria's smile, unburdened by wanting. The only pure thing he had found in this country.

He thought of his father. The traffic stop. The job interviews. The long years of being told he was too much and not enough.

He thought of the plane. The moment he stepped off, a millionaire, a free man, a future waiting.

The darkness was almost complete now. Just a pinprick of light remained, and in it, the faces of the women. Waiting. Always waiting.

Then the light went out.

End-of-Chapter Question: Can a place so beautiful be the death of you, and if so, is it the place or the people that make it a grave?

Chapter 12: The Wake

The body was found by a farmer named Boy, who came to the house that morning to report a problem with the irrigation pump. He knocked on the door, waited, knocked again. When no one answered, he walked around to the veranda, thinking Sir Norman might be sitting there, watching the fields as he often did at dawn.

The veranda was empty. But the door to the house was open.

Boy called out. No answer. He stepped inside, his feet hesitant on the marble floor, his heart already beating too fast. The house was quiet, too quiet, the kind of quiet that feels wrong, that makes the hair on your arms stand up.

He found Norman in the dining room.

Seated at the table, still, his head resting on his arms as if he had fallen asleep after a long meal. The remains of dinner were still there—plates, glasses, a half-empty bottle of wine. For a moment, Boy thought Sir Norman was simply resting. Then he saw the color of his skin. Not the warm brown of a living man, but something else. Something gray. Something finished.

Boy ran. He ran through the village, shouting, his voice cracking with fear and grief, and within an hour the house was full of people—neighbors, workers, the village captain, a policeman from the nearest town who happened to be visiting his mother.

The policeman's name was SPO2 Renato Cruz. He was a heavyset man with tired eyes and the patient air of someone who had seen too much to be surprised by anything. He walked through the house slowly, noting everything, touching nothing. He looked at the body, the plates, the glasses, the wine bottle. He looked at the kitchen, the bedrooms, the veranda. He asked questions, wrote answers in a small notebook, asked more questions.

By midday, the house was a crime scene.

The news spread through the village like fire through dry grass. Sir Norman was dead. Sir Norman had been murdered. Sir Norman, who built their school, their park, their community center. Sir Norman, who paved their roads and paid for their medicines and gave them jobs and hope and a future. Sir Norman was dead, and the women had done it.

Lola Puring was the first to say it aloud. She stood in the village square, surrounded by a crowd of shocked and grieving neighbors, and she spoke the words that everyone had been thinking but no one had dared to say.

"It was them. That family. The mother and her girls. I told him. I told him what they were, what they did, how they were raised. He didn't listen. He was too good, too trusting, too full of hope. And now he's dead, and they're laughing somewhere, counting his money, planning their next victim."

The crowd murmured. Some nodded. Some shook their heads, unwilling to believe. Some wept.

SPO2 Cruz arrived in the square, drawn by the noise. He listened to Lola Puring's accusations with the same patient expression he had worn all morning. Then he asked her to come to the police station, to make a formal statement, to tell him everything she knew.

She went willingly. She had been waiting her whole life to tell this story.

The arrest came at sunset.

The women were found at the mother's house, sitting calmly, as if they had been expecting visitors. Lilette. Her twin, whose name was Ligaya. The mother, Aling Belen. And two other women, girlfriends of the twins, who had been living in a small house not far from Norman's farm.

They did not resist. They did not protest. They simply gathered a few belongings, locked the door behind them, and walked with the policemen to the waiting vehicle. As she passed the village square, Lilette—or was it Ligaya?—

looked up and saw the crowd gathered there. Her face was calm, empty, unreadable. She did not speak. She did not wave. She just looked, for a long moment, at the people who had loved Norman, who had benefited from his generosity, who now stood in judgment of her.
Then she looked away, and the vehicle carried her out of the village, into the gathering dark.

The days that followed were a blur of investigation and grief.

SPO2 Cruz worked methodically, patiently, building a case from fragments. The testimony of Lola Puring. The records of Norman's bank transfers. The discovery of the down payment money, partially spent, partially hidden, in accounts controlled by the mother. The statements of villagers who had seen the women coming and going from Norman's house, who had noticed the switching, who had wondered but said nothing.

The autopsy confirmed what everyone suspected. Poison. A local toxin, derived from plants, slow-acting, untraceable in food. The kind of poison that country women had used for generations, on husbands who beat them, on lovers who betrayed them, on enemies who needed to disappear.

The women said nothing. They exercised their right to remain silent, sat in their cells, waited for whatever came next. Their faces through the bars were calm, empty, unbothered. They looked like women who had always known this day would come, who had accepted it as the price of the lives they had chosen.

The village mourned.

They held a vigil in the school stadium Norman had built. Hundreds of people came, carrying candles, singing hymns, weeping openly. They told stories of his kindness, his generosity, his simple decency. They remembered the roads he paved, the park he built, the millions he gave to the poor. They remembered the way he smiled at their children, the way he listened to their problems, the way he treated them not as inferiors but as equals.

Lola Puring spoke at the vigil. Her voice was strong, clear, unbroken by grief.

"He came here running from his own country," she said. "Running from people who hated him for the color of his skin. He thought he had found safety here. He thought he had found peace. He thought he had found love. Instead, he found us. And we failed him. Not all of us—some of us tried to warn him. But enough of us. Enough of us saw what was happening and said nothing. Enough of us let those women use him, drain him, destroy him. His blood is on our hands too."

The crowd was silent. The candles flickered in the darkness. Somewhere in the distance, a dog barked, and the rice fields rustled in the night breeze, indifferent to the grief of men.

Norman's body was prepared for burial. There was talk of sending him back to America, to Chicago, to the city he had fled. But the village petitioned to keep him. He belonged here, they said. This was his home now. These were his people. Let him rest in the soil he had loved, among the fields that had given him peace.

The authorities agreed. The American embassy was notified, paperwork was filed, permissions were granted. Norman Wright, son of Chicago, refugee from American racism, millionaire by accident of exchange rate, would be buried in the province he had adopted, among the people he had loved.

The funeral was on a Sunday.

The whole village came. They filled the church, spilled out into the yard, lined the road to the cemetery. They carried flowers, sang hymns, wept and prayed and said goodbye. The children from the school stadium formed an honor guard, their young faces solemn, their small hands clutching candles. The farmers he had worked with, the families he had helped, the old women who sat in his park—all of them came to see him home.

The coffin was simple, wooden, beautiful. It was carried by six men—farmers, workers, villagers who had known him, loved him, benefited from his generosity. They walked slowly, carefully, as if afraid of waking him.

At the graveside, under a sky the color of pearl, the priest spoke words of comfort and hope. He talked about the stranger who became a neighbor, the foreigner who became family, the man who gave everything and asked nothing in return. He talked about the mystery of evil, the tragedy of trust betrayed, the hope of justice beyond this world.

Then the coffin was lowered into the ground. The first handful of earth fell with a hollow sound. Then another. Then another.

The crowd began to disperse, drifting back to their homes, their fields, their lives. The children went first, their solemnity forgotten, already running and laughing. Then the women, talking quietly among themselves. Then the men, walking slowly, their faces heavy with thoughts they could not express.

Soon only Lola Puring remained.

She stood at the graveside, leaning on her cane, looking down at the fresh earth that covered the man she had tried to save. The wind moved through the rice fields, carrying the smell of growing things, the sound of distant water. The sun was warm on her old shoulders. The world continued, indifferent and eternal.

She thought of Norman. His smile. His kindness. His desperate hope. She thought of the women in their cells, waiting for trial, their faces calm and empty. She thought of the village, the country, the world—all the places where people used each other, hurt each other, destroyed each other, generation after generation, never learning, never changing.

She thought of the question he had asked her once, in a conversation she had almost forgotten. Can a man ever truly escape the history that shaped him?

She had not known the answer then. She did not know it now.

But standing there, in the silence of the cemetery, with the rice fields stretching to the horizon and the sky endless above, she thought she understood something. History was not a thing you escaped. It was a thing you carried. In your bones, in your blood, in the stories you told and the silences you kept. Norman had carried his history across an ocean, and it had followed him here, mingled with other histories, other hatreds, other wounds, and together they had killed him.

She turned away from the grave. The village waited, with its joys and sorrows, its kindnesses and cruelties, its ordinary life. She would go back to it, as she always did. She would sit in the park Norman built, watch the children play, remember the man who had given them everything and received a grave in return.

But first, she had one more thing to do.

She walked to the edge of the cemetery, where a small group of people stood waiting. Reporters, mostly, with their notebooks and cameras and hungry eyes. They had come from the city, drawn by the story—the rich American, the beautiful women, the poison, the betrayal. They wanted quotes, angles, explanations. They wanted to turn Norman's life into a headline, his death into a commodity.

Lola Puring looked at them. She saw their eagerness, their hunger, their complete inability to understand what had happened here. She saw the way they would simplify, distort, reduce a man's life to a few paragraphs, a few minutes of airtime. She saw the story they would tell, and she knew it would not be the truth.

But she also knew that truth was a fragile thing. It could not be captured in notebooks, preserved in photographs, contained in words. It lived in the hearts of those who had known him, in the memory of his smile, in the roads he paved and the school he built and the children who would grow up never knowing his name.

"He was a good man," she said to the reporters. "That is all you need to know."

She turned away from them and walked back towards the village, her slow steps carrying her away from the grave, away from the questions, away from the story they would tell. The rice fields shimmered in the afternoon light. The mountains stood blue in the distance. The world continued, beautiful and terrible, holding its secrets close.

Somewhere in a police station, three women sat in silence, waiting for justice or its absence. Somewhere in America, a city he had fled continued its indifferent hum. Somewhere in the province, a farmer bent over his field, planting rice, living the life Norman had loved.
And in the cemetery, under the fresh earth, a man lay still. A man who had crossed an ocean seeking freedom, who had found wealth and love and betrayal, who had given everything and received a grave. A man whose story would be told and retold, simplified and distorted, remembered and forgotten.

But for now, in this moment, he was simply Norman. A good man. That was all.

End-of-Chapter Question: When a man gives a community everything, and that community gives him a grave, whose story gets told—the giver's, or the taker's?

The End, for now

Appendix

347
Three Hundred and Forty-Seven

An essay on the weight we carry

I. The Number

Number 1.

It sits there on the page like a simple thing. Three. Four. Seven. You can say it in less than a second, write it in the time it takes to blink. But a number is not just a number when it counts years. And 347 years is not just a span of time. It is a wound that has never fully healed, a hemorrhage dressed with a Band-Aid and called cured.

From 1619, when the first enslaved Africans arrived at Point Comfort on the shores of Virginia, until 1865, when the last enslaved Black people in Galveston, Texas, finally learned they were free, the institution of chattel slavery existed on the soil of what would become the United States of America . Two hundred and forty-seven years. Longer than the United States has existed as a nation. Longer than any empire in the history of the West has lasted. A continuous, legally sanctioned, economically essential system of human bondage that treated people as property, as cargo, as things.

But the number, like all numbers, lies by being too small. It cannot convey the weight. It cannot convey the mothers who watched their children sold away, never to be seen again. The fathers who were worked to death in fields they would never own. The women whose bodies were not their own, used and discarded by masters who wrote laws to protect themselves from consequence. The families torn apart with the same casual efficiency that a farmer separates wheat from chaff. The 347 years are not just years. They are generations. Ten generations of Black people born into bondage, living in bondage, dying in bondage, their only legacy the blood and bone and sinew they poured into a country that counted them as three-fifths of a person and treated them as less.

American slavery was unique in the history of the world. Not because it was cruel—slavery has always been cruel. But because it was chattel slavery. The enslaved person was not a person with limited rights. The enslaved person was a thing. Property. An object that could be bought, sold, traded, insured, inherited, and disposed of at the owner's whim. This was codified in law, sanctified by religion, and enforced by violence. And because it was racial—because the slave was Black and the master was white—it created a hierarchy that did not end when the chains were removed. It became embedded in the DNA of the nation.

The 13th Amendment abolished slavery in 1865. But abolition is not the same as justice. Freedom is not the same as equality. The chains were removed, but the scars remained. And the architects of white supremacy, defeated on the battlefield, simply retreated to the statehouses and began to build a new system of control.

They called it Jim Crow.

II. The Crow and the Crow

The name came from a minstrel show. A white actor in blackface makeup, dancing and singing a caricature of Blackness, calling himself "Jim Crow." It was meant to be funny. It was meant to demean. And by the end of the 19th century, it had become the name for the most comprehensive system of racial subjugation the world had ever seen.

Jim Crow was not a single law. It was a thousand laws, a million customs, an entire way of life built on the premise that Black people were inferior and must be kept separate, subordinate, and silent. From the 1870s until 1965, these laws governed every aspect of life in the American South and beyond.

They segregated everything. Schools. Hospitals. Restaurants. Water fountains. Bathrooms. Buses. Trains. Parks. Beaches. Swimming pools. Libraries. Cemeteries.

In some cities, it was illegal for Black and white people to play checkers together. In others, textbooks could not be shared across the color line. In Oklahoma, the law required separate phone booths . The logic was relentless, absurd, and deadly serious.

The Supreme Court blessed this system in 1896 with Plessy v. Ferguson, enshrining the doctrine of "separate but equal" into constitutional law . But the facilities were never equal. Black schools received a fraction of the funding of white schools. Black hospitals were understaffed and underfunded. Black neighborhoods were denied basic services. The "equal" part of "separate but equal" was a lie told to justify the separation.

And then there was the vote.

The 15th Amendment had guaranteed Black men the right to vote in 1870 . But the Jim Crow South found ways around it. Poll taxes required poor Black sharecroppers to pay fees they could not afford. Literacy tests asked impossible questions, required interpretation of arcane legal texts, or simply failed Black applicants regardless of their answers. Grandfather clauses said that if your grandfather had voted before the Civil War— which no Black grandfather had—you could vote regardless of literacy . The result was devastating. In Louisiana, 130,000 Black voters were registered in 1896. By 1904, there were 1,342 . In Mississippi, fewer than

9,000 of 147,000 voting-age Black citizens were registered . An entire population, stripped of political voice.

And behind the laws stood the lynch mobs.

Between 1877 and 1950, more than 4,000 Black Americans were lynched in the United States . They were hanged from trees, burned alive, shot, beaten, mutilated—often in front of cheering crowds that included women and children, sometimes photographed and turned into postcards. The victims were accused of crimes real and imagined. Mostly they were accused of the crime of being Black in a world that had decided Blackness was a capital offense. No one was ever convicted for most of these murders. The killers walked free, often celebrated as heroes.

This was Jim Crow. A system of total control. A regime of terror. A hundred years of legalized white supremacy, enforced by law and custom and violence, designed to keep Black Americans in a state of perpetual subjugation.

And the women? They bore a double burden.

The term "Jane Crow" emerged to describe what Black women experienced—the intersection of racial oppression and sexual subjugation . They were not just Black in a world that hated Blackness. They were women in a world that treated women as property. They were vulnerable to sexual violence in ways that white women were not, with no legal recourse, no protection, no justice. The men who raped them were rarely punished. The children born of those rapes were often sold. The pain of Black women under Jim Crow is a story within a story, a wound within a wound, too often forgotten in the telling of the larger horror.

III. The Tapestry

The Civil Rights Act of 1964 and the Voting Rights Act of 1965 struck down the legal framework of Jim Crow . The laws were gone. The signs came down. The water fountains were integrated. The schools were desegregated. The voting booths were opened.

But the damage was done.

Four hundred and forty-seven years, if you count from the first enslaved Africans to the present. Two hundred and forty-seven of slavery. One hundred of Jim Crow. And then fifty-something years of something else—a time when the laws are equal but the playing field is not.

The effects remain. They are woven into the tapestry of America, threads of darkness in a fabric that likes to pretend it is only red, white, and blue.
Look at the wealth gap. The typical white family today has eight times the wealth of the typical Black family .

This is not an accident. It is the direct result of centuries of theft—of labor stolen during slavery, of land stolen during Reconstruction, of homes stolen through redlining, of education stolen through underfunded schools, of opportunity stolen through discrimination in hiring and promotion. When white families were building equity through the GI Bill and federally subsidized mortgages, Black families were locked out by law and practice. The wealth that white families passed down to their children came, in part, from a system that prevented Black families from building wealth at all.

Look at the criminal justice system. Black Americans are incarcerated at more than five times the rate of white Americans . The War on Drugs, declared in the 1980s, targeted Black communities with a ferocity it never applied to white suburbs, despite comparable rates of drug use. The school-to-prison pipeline pushes Black children out of classrooms and into cells. The police kill Black men at disproportionate rates, and the officers almost never face consequences . The Thirteenth Amendment abolished slavery "except as a punishment for crime." That exception has been exploited to create a new system of forced labor, a new caste, a new form of control that looks different from Jim Crow but feels the same to those caught in its gears.

Look at housing. The practice of redlining—explicitly denying mortgages and insurance to Black neighborhoods—was government policy for decades. When it was outlawed, the damage was done. Black families had been locked out of the greatest wealth-building opportunity in American history: home ownership. The neighborhoods that were redlined are still poorer, still more segregated, still denied the investment that white neighborhoods received as a matter of course. The segregation that was once mandated by law is now maintained by economics, by custom, by the simple fact that if you have no wealth, you cannot move to where the wealth is.

Look at health care. Black mothers die from pregnancy-related causes at three times the rate of white mothers. Black infants die at twice the rate of white infants. Black Americans have higher rates of diabetes, heart disease, hypertension, and nearly every other chronic condition. They receive less pain medication, less aggressive treatment, less compassionate care. The stress of living in a body that the world has decided is worth less—the "weathering" effect, scholars call it—ages Black bodies prematurely, wears them down, kills them young.

Look at education. Schools are more segregated today than they were in the 1970s. The promise of Brown v. Board of Education has not been fulfilled. Black children attend schools with fewer resources, less experienced teachers, and lower expectations. They are disciplined more harshly for the same behaviors. They are pushed into special education and out of gifted programs. The achievement gap is not a mystery. It is the direct result of a system that has never truly committed to educating Black children.

Look at employment. A Black man with a college degree has the same chance of getting a job as a white man with a high school diploma . "Black-sounding" names on resumes receive 50% fewer callbacks than identical resumes with "white-sounding" names. The discrimination is not always explicit. It doesn't have to be. It is built into the networks, the assumptions, the unconscious biases of a society that has spent 400 years learning to see Blackness as less.

Look at the recent attempts to dismantle diversity, equity, and inclusion programs . Look at the efforts to ban the teaching of critical race theory, to sanitize history, to pretend that slavery and Jim Crow were aberrations rather than foundations. Look at the laws being passed to restrict voting access, targeting the very communities that were once targeted by poll taxes and literacy tests. The names change. The methods change. The goal remains the same.

This is the tapestry. Threads of progress woven with threads of resistance. Moments of hope followed by seasons of backlash. A nation that declared "all men are created equal" while holding millions in bondage. A nation that fought a civil war over slavery and then spent the next century finding new ways to maintain white supremacy. A nation that elected a Black president and then, eight years later, saw a resurgence of open white nationalism.

The low-grade fever that Norman Wright carried in his bones—that all Black Americans carry in their bones—is not just memory. It is the present. It is the knowledge that the system that enslaved your ancestors and terrorized your grandparents and discriminated against your parents is not gone. It has just changed its name, changed its tactics, changed its face.

IV. The Question

Is it possible to escape?

Norman asked this question at the end of Chapter One, standing on the edge of his American life, about to step onto a plane that would carry him halfway around the world. Can a man ever truly escape the history that shaped him, or does he carry it in his bones like a low-grade fever?

The answer, as he discovered, is complicated.

You can leave the country. You can cross an ocean. You can trade your dollars for pesos and become a millionaire overnight. You can build a mansion in the rice fields and pave roads and build schools and become a beloved figure in a village that has never seen anyone like you. You can fall in love, or what feels like love. You can build a life, or what feels like a life.

But you cannot leave your bones behind. You cannot shed the history that lives in your cells, the caution that your father taught you, the knowledge that the world is not safe for people who look like you. That knowledge is not paranoia. It is wisdom, hard-earned over centuries, passed down through generations, encoded in the very structure of Black American consciousness.

Norman's tragedy was not that he trusted the wrong people, though he did. It was not that he fell in love with a woman who was using him, though he did. It was that he tried to escape his history by running from it, rather than understanding that history goes where you go. It is in your blood. It is in your bones. It is in the way you see the world and the way the world sees you, no matter how far you travel.

The Philippines was not America. The women who smiled at Norman were not the cops who threw him against his car. But the low-grade fever did not care about geography. It was with him on the plane, with him in the rice field, with him in the mansion, with him at the dinner table where he ate his last meal. It was with him when he died.

The question is not whether you can escape. The question is whether you can learn to live with what you carry. Whether you can find a way to transform the fever into something else—into awareness, into caution, into wisdom, into love that sees clearly rather than love that hopes desperately. Whether you can build something real on ground that has been poisoned by history, knowing that the poison is still there, but also knowing that things can grow anyway.

Norman did not figure this out in time. He was too lonely, too hopeful, too desperate to be loved. He wanted so badly to believe that he had found a home that he ignored every sign that the home was a trap. He wanted so badly to believe that he was loved that he refused to see the women who were loving him to death.

His story is a warning. But it is also a mirror. Because every Black American who reads it will recognize something of themselves in Norman. The hope. The caution. The desperate desire to find a place where the fever breaks. The knowledge, deep down, that the fever never breaks. It just changes. It just waits. It just is.

347 years. And counting.

For Norman. For all the Normans. For the ones who found peace and the ones who found graves and the ones still looking, still hoping, still carrying the fever in their bones.

Character Study

The Names We Carry: A Meditation on Symbol, Shadow, and the Weight of Becoming

I. Norman Wright: The Normal Man, The Right Man

His name is not an accident.

Norman. From the Old English norþ and mann—north man. But the word has traveled further than its etymology. In modern usage, "normal" means ordinary, average, unexceptional. The kind of man you pass on the street without noticing. The kind of man who lives his life, pays his taxes, loves his family, and dies without making headlines. Norman Wright is, by name, the everyman. The human being stripped of particularity, the universal soul trying to find his way through a world that keeps telling him he doesn't belong.

And Wright. Not just a surname, but a declaration. Right. Correct. Just. The man who tries to do the right thing, who believes in right and wrong, who carries within him a moral compass that he assumes everyone else shares. He is right in another sense too—right as opposed to left, the dominant hand, the hand that does the work, the hand that reaches out to others. He is the man who extends himself, who gives, who builds, who trusts.

Norman Wright is you. He is me. He is anyone who has ever hoped for better, believed in love, trusted a smile. He is the universal human desire to belong, to matter, to be seen and loved for who we are. His Blackness is specific—it shapes his history, his caution, his fever—but his humanity is universal. He wants what we all want. He loses what we all fear losing. He dies because he hoped, and hoping made him blind.

The tragedy of Norman Wright is not that he was different. It is that he was exactly the same as every one of us. He wanted to believe. And the world, in its cruelty, gave him reason to.

II. Maria: The Blessed Among Women

In a novel saturated with betrayal, Maria is the single point of light.

Her name is not an accident either. Maria is the Spanish and Filipino form of Mary, the mother of Jesus, the Blessed Virgin, the Theotokos—God-bearer. In the Philippines, a nation shaped by centuries of Spanish Catholicism, the name carries weight that Americans can barely comprehend. The Virgin Mary is everywhere—in churches, in homes, in tricycles, in the po and opo of respectful speech, in the Pasyon sung during Holy Week, in the Flores de Mayo celebrated by children. She is the ideal of womanhood: pure, compassionate, self-sacrificing, the mother who intercedes for her children, the refuge of sinners, the comforter of the afflicted.

Maria the translator embodies this ideal, but she is not a caricature. She is not the Virgin descended to earth. She is a young woman with bare feet and a textbook and dreams of escaping the poverty that has trapped her family for generations. But she is also what her name suggests: a source of grace in Norman's life, the one person who sees him clearly and gives him the truth, even when the truth hurts.

She does not use him. She does not manipulate him. She does not pretend to love him to get what she wants. When Norman confesses his feelings, she gently, kindly refuses him—not because she is cruel, but because she is honest. She knows what she needs, and she knows he is not it. That honesty is the purest gift she could give him, and he is too blind to see it until it is too late.

Maria is what the other women in this story could have been. She is the path not taken, the choice not made, the possibility of something real in a world of performance. Her name blesses her, but her circumstances do not. She is poor, struggling, dreaming of escape. But she has not let her suffering sour into cruelty. She has not let the abuses of the past become the weapons of the future. She has resisted the temptation that destroys the other women—the temptation to become what hurt her.

In a Catholic country, she is the saint who walks among sinners. And Norman, like so many before him, fails to recognize the saint when she stands before him.

III. The Trinity of Shadows: Grandmother, Mother, Daughters

If Maria is the Blessed Virgin, the other women are her shadow. They form a trinity—not holy, but unholy; not redemptive, but destructive; not a source of grace, but a well of poison.

The Grandmother. The Mother. The Daughters (the twins).

Three generations. Three wounds. Three women bound together by blood and by the hatred that blood has carried like a virus. They are not born evil. They are made evil, forged in the crucible of abuse, shaped by men who hurt them, used them, discarded them. The grandmother was beaten by her husband, left with nothing but children and debt. The mother was beaten by hers, abandoned to drugs and despair. The twins watched this, learned from this, became this.

Their hatred is not abstract. It is personal, specific, earned. Men took everything from them. Men gave them nothing but pain. And so men became the enemy, not as an idea but as a fact, as a truth written on their bodies and in their memories. The society of women they build is a fortress against a world that has only ever hurt them. And Norman, poor Norman, is just another invader approaching the gates.

But here is the tragedy within the tragedy: they do not simply defend themselves. They attack. They do not simply protect each other. They prey on others. They become the very thing that hurt them—predators, users, destroyers. The abused become abusers, not because they are evil, but because they have never been shown another way. The crucible that forged them was fire, and fire is all they know how to make.

The grandmother taught the mother. The mother taught the daughters. The lessons were survival, but survival became cruelty, and cruelty became a way of life. They are a trinity of inherited evil, each generation passing down the poison like a heirloom, like a curse, like the only thing of value they have to give.

IV. The Timeless Language: No Past, No Future, Only Now
There is a detail about the Philippines that changes everything, if you let it.

The languages of the archipelago—Cebuano, Tagalog, Ilocano, and dozens of others—do not conjugate verbs for tense the way English does. They have markers for time, yes, words that indicate when something happened or will happen. But the verbs themselves remain unchanged. The action is the same whether it occurred yesterday, is occurring today, or will occur tomorrow.

This is not just grammar. It is a way of seeing the world.

In a language without tense, the past is not truly past. It is present, always present, folded into the now, inseparable from the moment. What happened to your grandmother is not a memory. It is a reality, as real as the food on your table, as the roof over your head, as the man sitting across from you. The abuse does not recede into history. It continues, always, because the language does not allow it to be placed in the past.

For the women in this story, this linguistic truth is also a psychological truth. The beatings their grandmother endured are not over. They are still happening, every time a man raises his hand, every time a man looks at them with desire, every time a man says he loves them. The abandonment their mother suffered is not finished. It is still happening, every time a man leaves, every time a man promises and fails to deliver, every time a man proves himself untrustworthy. The pain is not in the past. It is in the present, always in the present, because the language does not allow it to be anywhere else.

This is why they cannot stop. This is why they cannot choose differently. The abuse is not something that happened to them. It is something that is happening to them, continuously, eternally, every moment of every day. And the only way they have found to fight back is to do to others what was done to them.

Norman, with his English tenses and his linear view of time, cannot understand this. He thinks the past is past. He thinks wounds heal. He thinks people can move on. He does not realize that he has entered a world where time moves differently, where the past is never over, where every man is every man who ever hurt them, and every betrayal is justified before it even begins.

V. The Crucible and the Choice

The crucible is real. The abuse is real. The pain is real.

But the choice remains.

Maria faced the same crucible. She grew up in the same poverty, witnessed the same suffering, carried the same history. Her grandmother may have been beaten. Her mother may have been abandoned. She may have seen things no child should see, endured things no person should endure. But she did not become what hurt her. She chose differently.

Why?

The novel does not answer this question. Perhaps it cannot. Perhaps the mystery of why some people survive their pain without becoming poison is as deep as the mystery of why others are consumed by it. But Maria stands as a witness, a reminder that the cycle can be broken, that the abused do not have to become abusers, that the past does not have to determine the future.

She is the blessed among women not because she is perfect, but because she chose. She chose honesty over manipulation, clarity over confusion, friendship over exploitation. She chose to see Norman as a person, not a resource. She chose to give him the truth, even when the truth cost her something—a protector, a provider, a path out of poverty.

The other women chose differently. They chose survival at any cost. They chose to become what hurt them. They chose to pass the poison down, generation after generation, a trinity of shadows bound together by blood and by the hatred that blood now carries.

Norman, caught between them, never stood a chance. He was too hopeful, too lonely, too desperate to be loved. He saw Maria and thought she was a possibility. He saw Lilette and thought she was the answer. He never understood that they were the same question, asked in different ways.

The question is this: Can you carry your history without becoming your history? Can you bear the weight of what was done to you without doing it to someone else? Can you suffer and still choose love, still choose trust, still choose to be the person you were before the world broke you?

Maria says yes. The other women say no. And Norman, poor Norman, just wanted to be loved.

Is that so wrong?

Is that so human?

Is that not all any of us want?

VI. The Fever

Norman carries the fever of his history—347 years of slavery and Jim Crow, of being told he is too much and not enough, of traffic stops and overqualified verdicts and a country that was built on his ancestors' bones and has never stopped reminding him of it. That fever is real. It is in his bones, in his blood, in the way he sees the world and the way the world sees him.

The women carry their own fever—generations of abuse, of men who hurt them and left them, of a language that keeps the pain always present, always now. That fever is just as real. It is in their bones too, in their blood, in the way they see men and the way men have taught them to see.

Two fevers. Two histories. Two sets of wounds, colliding in a rice field on the other side of the world.
Norman's fever makes him cautious, but also desperate. He has been hurt so long that he is willing to ignore new hurts for the promise of love. The women's fever makes them wary, but also predatory. They have been hurt so long that hurting others feels like justice, like survival, like the only language they know.

Neither fever is their fault. Both fevers are real. But fevers, left untreated, kill. They kill the one who carries them and sometimes, if the fever is hot enough, they kill the ones nearby.

Norman died because he hoped. The women killed him because they could not stop hurting. Maria lived because she chose differently.

The names matter. Norman—the normal man, the right man, the everyman. Maria—the blessed woman, the source of grace, the possibility of redemption. The others—the grandmother, the mother, the daughters—they are not named for what they could be. They are named for what they became. And what they became is a warning.

The abused must resist the tendency to become abusers. The wounded must resist the temptation to wound others. The fever must be treated, not passed on.

Otherwise, the cycle continues. Otherwise, the poison spreads. Otherwise, normal men die in rice fields, killed by women who were once girls, who were once innocent, who were once just like Maria.

And the language, having no tense, cannot even say that it is over.

It is always now. Always happening. Always.

For Norman. For Maria. For the grandmother, the mother, the daughters. For all of us, carrying our fevers, trying to find a way to break the cycle before it breaks us.

The Disease We Pass Down: A Meditation on Violence and the Golden Rule

There is a rule so simple, so ancient, so universal that it appears in nearly every culture, every faith, every moral tradition on earth. Do unto others as you would have them do unto you. Treat others as you wish to be treated. Love your neighbor as yourself.

The Golden Rule.

It seems obvious. Obvious as breathing, obvious as sunrise. And yet, generation after generation, we fail to live it. We hurt the ones closest to us. We strike out in anger. We use words as weapons. We exploit the power we hold over those who are smaller, weaker, more vulnerable. And then we wonder why the world is broken.

Violence against another person—whether physical, verbal, or emotional—is violence against ourselves. Because we are connected. Because the hand that strikes also belongs to the body that bleeds. Because the word that wounds also belongs to the mouth that speaks. Because the family that tears itself apart leaves no one whole.

This is not metaphor. This is biology, psychology, sociology, spirit.

The Generational Curse

In families, violence is a disease. It spreads not through germs but through example, through normalization, through the slow poison of "this is just how it is." A child who witnesses violence learns that violence is how problems are solved. A child who is hit learns that hitting is love, or discipline, or simply what adults do. A child who is screamed at learns that screaming is communication.

And then that child grows up. And becomes a parent. And the cycle continues.

Poor mental health feeds this disease. Depression, anxiety, unresolved trauma, unhealed wounds—they fester and spread. A person who does not love themselves cannot truly love another. A person who has never been shown kindness cannot easily show kindness. The disease passes down, generation to generation, until someone has the courage to say: Stop. This ends with me.

The Unfair Advantage

We must also speak honestly about power.

The dynamic between men and women is often unbalanced. Men are physically stronger, on average. Men have been socially conditioned to dominate, to control, to assert. Women have been conditioned to submit, to endure, to forgive. This is not natural. This is learned. And it can be unlearned.

The dynamic between adults and children is even more stark. Children are completely vulnerable, completely dependent. They have no voice, no choice, no escape. When an adult uses that power to hurt—to hit, to yell, to manipulate—it is not discipline. It is not teaching. It is abuse. And the child carries that abuse forever.

Verbal abuse leaves no bruises. No scars. No evidence. But it damages just as deeply. The words we speak to our partners, our children, our siblings, our parents—they echo. They become the voices in the head. They become the stories we tell ourselves about who we are. Choose your words as carefully as you would choose medicine for a wound.

What Goes Around

There is another ancient truth, found in every wisdom tradition: you reap what you sow. What goes around comes around. The energy you put into the world returns to you, multiplied.

This is not about punishment. It is about consequence. A family built on fear will produce children who fear. A relationship built on control will produce partners who rebel or collapse. A life built on hurting others will produce a self that is hollow, lonely, broken.

But the reverse is also true. A family built on kindness produces children who are kind. A relationship built on respect produces partners who thrive. A life built on love produces a self that is whole.

Help Is Not Weakness

We seek help for our bodies without shame. We see doctors for heart disease. We take medication for high blood pressure. We change our diets to avoid diabetes. Why should our hearts—our spiritual, emotional, mental hearts—be any different?

If you are angry, seek help. If you are hurting, seek help. If you find yourself raising a hand, raising your voice, raising walls between yourself and those you love—seek help. There is no shame in this. The shame is in refusing, in continuing, in passing the disease to the next generation.

Therapists, counselors, support groups, faith leaders, trusted friends—they exist for a reason. They are the doctors for the broken heart. Use them.

A Final Word

The Golden Rule is not complicated. It is not demanding. It simply asks: How do you want to be treated?

With kindness? Then be kind.

With gentleness? Then be gentle.

With respect? Then be respectful.

With love? Then love.

This is the only cure for the disease of violence. This is the only way to break the chain. This is the only hope for the generations to come.

Treat others as you wish to be treated. Love others as you wish to be loved. Because violence against them is violence against yourself. Because healing them is healing yourself. Because we are all connected—partners, friends, foreigners, siblings, strangers—and what we do to one another, we do to us all.

For Norman. For every victim of violence. For every survivor. For every person trying to break the cycle. You are not alone. Help exists. Choose it.

Resources:

· National Domestic Violence Hotline (US): 1-800-799-7233
· Philippines National Anti-Violence Against Women and Children Hotline: 1343
· International Directory of Domestic Violence Agencies: www.hotpeachpages.net

Acknowledgment: Margie's Legacy

To my grandmother, Margie.

She gave me pure love. In a world that had given her so much less, she somehow found more than enough to give to me. I watched her endure what no one should endure—violence by the hands and voice of the man who should have protected her. I watched her carry wounds I will never fully know.

And still, she loved me.

She did not let bitterness take root in the space where her gentleness lived. She did not let the poison pass to me. She held me, taught me, shaped me. From her I learned what it means to be community. To take care of family. To look after neighbors. To give what you have, even when you have little. Especially when you have little.

Everything I am, everything I have become, everything I know about love—it all begins with her. She is not just in my memory. She is in my hands, my voice, my way of moving through the world. She is in this book, in every page, in every question about love and trust and the people we choose to become.

I am her legacy. That is the greatest honor of my life.

This story—this warning, this meditation, this prayer—it is for her too. For the grandmothers who endured. For the children who watched. For the ones who broke the

cycle and the ones still trying. For everyone carrying wounds and choosing, anyway, to love.
Thank you, Margie. For everything.

You are remembered.
You are honored.
You are loved.

Placement Note: This acknowledgment appears in the Appendix alongside the anti-domestic violence article, creating a powerful pairing—the universal message followed by the personal testament. Together they form a complete statement: This is what I learned. This is why it matters. This is who taught me.

About the author

Tito Santos, born in Merida in 1965, is a celebrated Hispanic-American writer known for his deeply reflective and poignant narratives. Raised in a modest household, Tito developed an early love for storytelling through his grandmother's tales of Maya Mythology. His passion for language flourished, leading him to pursue studies in literature and history, which informed his unique perspective on identity, culture, and social justice.

Tito's works often explore themes of personal conflict, migration, and imaginative experiences that give voice to characters navigating complex relationships and societal expectations. His novella Letters to Her marked his literary debut under the pseudonym, capturing intimate reflections on love, loss, and transformation.

Despite his success, Tito remains reclusive, living a quiet life as a citizen of the World, where he finds inspiration in nature and the diverse stories of immigrant communities. A fierce advocate for marginalized voices, he donates a portion of his book royalties to causes supporting education and human rights across the globe.

Holam is a Hebrew niqqud vowel sign, represented as a dot above the upper left corner of a consonant. It makes no sound of its own. A holam determines the sound of another letter; it gives voice to the consonant that it joins in partnership.

Made in the USA
Coppell, TX
02 March 2026

72693263R00085